EVERYWHERE YOU DON'T BELONG

EVERYWHERE
YOU DON'T BELONG

A NOVEL BY

Gabriel Bump

ALGONQUIN BOOKS OF CHAPEL HILL 2020

Published by
ALGONQUIN BOOKS OF CHAPEL HILL
Post Office Box 2225
Chapel Hill, North Carolina 27515-2225

a division of
WORKMAN PUBLISHING
225 Varick Street
New York, New York 10014

LIBRARY OF CONGRESS CATALOGING-IN-PUBLICATION DATA

Names: Bump, Gabriel, author.
Title: Everywhere you don't belong / a novel by Gabriel Bump.
Other titles: Everywhere you do not belong
Description: First edition. | Chapel Hill, North Carolina :
Algonquin Books of Chapel Hill, [2020]
Identifiers: LCCN 2019008323 | ISBN 9781616208790 (hardcover : alk. paper)
Classification: LCC PS3602.U474 E95 2020 | DDC 813/.6—dc23
LC record available at https://lccn.loc.gov/2019008323

10 9 8 7 6 5 4 3 2 1
First Edition

For Grandma

EVERYWHERE YOU DON'T BELONG

PART ONE

///////////////////////////////

South Shore

Euclid Avenue

"IF THERE'S ONE thing wrong with people," Paul always said, "it's that no one remembers the shit that they should, and everyone remembers the shit that doesn't matter for shit."

I remember Euclid Avenue. I remember yelling outside our window, coming in from the street. Grandma putting down her coffee. I remember Grandma holding my ankle, swinging my two-year-old self out the front door, flipping me right-side up, plopping me down next to the Hawaiian violets, plopping herself down next to me. I remember awe and disbelief.

Dad was on the curb, wrestling another man. He had the man's head, the man's life and soul, between his thighs.

Upstairs, above our heads, Mom screamed for the men to stop, to regain their senses, civilize themselves.

"You're friends!" Mom yelled. "You go to church!"

"Say it again," Dad told the man.

"I'm sorry," the man told Dad.

"Sorry for what?" Dad asked the man.

"Sorry for saying you look like Booker T. Washington," the man told Dad.

Dad loosened his grip on the man. Chicago cops came speeding down our street before Dad's loafer could dislodge the man's teeth.

"Gentlemen," Dad told the cops, after noticing me sitting there, applauding. "Not in front of my son."

The cops shook their heads at this ridiculous black-on-black crime.

"You're brothers," the cops said. "You're on the same side."

The man on the ground stood up, brushed grass and dirt off his jeans, wiped his bloody and twisted nose on his torn shirtsleeve, adjusted his purple and blue floral tie, adjusted his large silver belt buckle. He stared at me, this man I hadn't seen before and would never see again. He had a sad face. On his tongue: something important and tragic, a forever-buried secret.

Then Paul ran out with a fireplace poker, with his robe open and his belly fat rippling.

"That's it," Grandma said. "Enough culture for one day."

No one pressed charges. When the cops came around asking, no one had seen anything. It never happened.

Fog

////////

DAD'S FRIENDS HUNG out in places I couldn't go, on the other side of the tracks, down Jeffrey Avenue, deeper into South Shore. That's where Dad grew up, near the train stop to Indiana, across from the strip mall. That's where Dad's friends lived, still, in apartments clustered near mass transportation—people always coming and going and waiting and never leaving.

Mom was from the Highlands, a three-block chunk of South Shore reserved for black doctors, black politicians, black bankers, and black lawyers—all the rich people too dark-skinned for the suburbs, too poor to live downtown.

Dad's friends didn't come over often.

In the sixties, when they were teenagers, Coach and Dad had tipped buckets.

They snuck up and tipped buckets of fish in the harbor, hauling ass through the golf course before the guy in a Vienna Beef uniform could catch them. That was when South Shore was still Jewish and Irish, before expressways and White Flight and manicured suburbs.

When the guy in a Vienna Beef uniform caught Dad, he dangled Dad by his ankles over the harbor and promised to drown him. There was a moral to that story, but Dad was never sure what it was. Coach thought the moral was don't fuck with anybody in a Vienna Beef uniform.

When they were growing up, Harold Washington was mayor. The Jews and Irish were almost gone. A few stubborn old men refused to leave, clung to their porches until death, didn't care about the neighborhood's changing color. Dad and Coach would recite poetry by the water. Dad, once, wanted to get a doctorate in high Renaissance art. Coach, once, wanted to play in Northern Italy, make a modest living around high culture.

When they were young, Dad and Coach rode their bikes through the Highlands.

When Dad started taking me to see Coach, Mom thought Dad was toughening me up by letting me witness a broken man break further. There wasn't anything tough about Coach. His wife had left him with two babies and moved to Florida. Dad took me to see Coach because Dad thought Coach was capable of murder-suicide.

The first time Dad took me to Coach's apartment, five of us

sat in three plastic chairs on Coach's shag rug. Dad bounced the babies on his knees.

The empty fireplace overflowed with dusty trophies. When Coach started crying, Dad made me go into the bedroom with the babies.

ONE THANKSGIVING WHEN I was five, Dad invited Coach over. Paul sat in the living room, watched Detroit struggle against Green Bay, and grunted when Coach pushed the double-wide pink stroller through the door.

"Paul," Coach said. Paul was Grandma's friend.

Coach handed the babies off to Mom and sat next to Paul on the couch.

The game was enough to get Coach and Paul drunk off excitement. Dad wanted to get drunk too. Mom and Grandma kept yelling from the kitchen.

Dad gave me a beer at dinner, which turned into a fight.

"What do you want my grandson to be?" Grandma said.

"What do you want our son to be?" Mom said.

"This is a party, and I don't want him to feel left out," Dad said.

"My grandson is not a follower," Grandma said. "He is his own man."

"My son will be a force in the world," Mom said.

"A father can give his son a beer whenever he wants. I can give my son a beer whenever I want." Dad slammed the table.

Nobody looked at me. While they argued, I chugged the beer as fast as possible. Grandma, Mom, and Dad looked at Coach, who was flinging mashed potatoes at a giggling Paul. He used his fork as a slingshot. Mom slammed the table. Paul wiped the potatoes from his face. Coach turned toward Mom, raised his weapon, and hit Mom on the neck so clumps fell down her blouse. Grandma gasped while laughing. Her bracelets jingled when she grabbed her chest. Dad went for another beer. Paul called Coach a bastard. I felt lightheaded and sick.

The babies' crying marked the end of Thanksgiving. Mom held open the front door, held back her own tears. Dad told me to get my coat.

Jeffrey Avenue felt quiet. Cars dodged potholes with grace. Coach stood at the stoplight and didn't say a word. We all smiled, waited for the light to change, looked at a bus struggle to a stop, and nodded at the faces in the window.

Outside Coach's building, I knelt in front of the babies. Dad grabbed Coach behind his neck.

"Are you going to be okay?" Dad said.

"Can you come upstairs?" Coach asked. "Please."

Dad carried the babies. I folded the stroller and lugged it up. Coach hummed like mad over his jangling keys.

Who said, "God hates me"? Who opened the bottle? Who sat there drinking all night and paced around the room with arms raised toward the ceiling and asked for forgiveness? Who forgot I was standing there? Who didn't hear the babies crying?

Dad woke up the next day with a hangover.

Coach disappeared around Christmas.

The babies ended up in Kentucky, or Pennsylvania.

And my life went on like that: people coming and going, valuable things left in a hurry.

Sixty-Third Street Beach

When Mom and Dad had their final fight, we were late to an all-black rendition of *Fiddler on the Roof*.

"Fuck Hakeem Olajuwon!" Dad screamed from the dark water.

Dad was out there without a boat, without pants or suit jacket, down to his underwear, past the buoy, rocking with the swells, pumping his arms up and down, jamming to the news— Jordan was coming back. No more baseball. Back to work. Back to the 'ship.

There was a storm coming up the horizon, up from Indiana. Lightning hit that junk barge, that barge always floating on Lake Michigan.

I was out there on the beach, in my nice shoes, stumbling,

messing up my nice pants, yelling for my family to stabilize, relax, act normal.

I remember Mom with her dangling earrings. Her bracelets had rubies. Her necklace was sapphire and thick. I remember her near the shore, running, jangling, not caring about broken glass, kicking up sand, not caring about her hair, her shoes, her dress—the final straw.

"Claude," Grandma called from the parking lot. "Fly your behind back over here."

"Join me!" Dad yelled to all of us.

"You'll die!" Mom yelled back.

"Fuck Olajuwon!" Dad yelled to heaven.

"We'll miss the first act!" Mom yelled to a separate and more desperate heaven.

Grandma pulled me into the back seat between her and Paul.

"It's just a game," Paul said. Paul was a Knicks fan.

Grandma got my cheek between her thumb and middle finger. She squeezed and pulled our faces close. Her long false lashes brushed against my eyebrows. Her lipstick, from that close: clumped and peeling, cracked. She wasn't scared; she was hard; she knew.

I don't remember how she smelled; I don't remember what she said. I remember looking past her moving lips. Out there: my father, still past the buoy, still waving his arms, still floating, still here.

The next day, Mom left us and Euclid Avenue and Sixty-Third

Street beach. The day after that, Dad followed her. Neither left a note or kiss goodbye.

"That's it," Paul said, then, in the car, before pulling a sleeping mask from his breast pocket. "That's enough culture for one day."

We missed the first and second acts; we missed the play.

Bubbly and Nugget

//

MS. BEV ASKED if our parents loved us. She was crying again. We always said yes when she cried. When the divorce started she brought three lunches to class, eating them throughout the day.

"That's good," she said. "Love is good."

She put her head on the table and bid us to leave. We were nine. We didn't have anywhere to go. There was a foot of snow outside.

Bubbly leaned over and whispered to me. "I think she's going to kill herself."

"How do you kill yourself?" I asked. I loved Bubbly.

She stuck a finger up her nose and ate what she found.

"My parents think she's going to kill herself," she said.

Nugget smiled, showed us an eraser in his mouth.

"She's just sad," Nugget said over the eraser, spit coming down his chin. "Haven't you guys ever been sad?"

Bubbly raised a fist at Nugget. Fear confused Nugget. Back then, he couldn't tell fear from sadness. When he got older he found out. He jumped out of a plane. His parachute didn't open. It was on the news.

He took the eraser out of his mouth and rolled it between his palms.

"Nugget," Bubbly said, "you smell like bologna."

"Thank you," he said, and turned around. Nugget loved bologna.

"You're nice," I said to Bubbly.

I was going to ask Bubbly to marry me, but Principal Big Ass walked in. His real name was Gene Longley IV.

"Mrs. Beverley," Principal Big Ass said. "May I speak with you in the hall?"

"It's Ms. Bev," Nugget said.

"What was that, Jeffrey?" Principal Big Ass asked.

"It's Nugget," Bubbly said.

"What, Tiffany?" he asked.

"It's Bubbly," I said.

"Claude?" His face turned purple.

"Yeah, that's right," Nugget said. Everybody laughed. Nugget put the eraser back in his mouth.

I didn't want a nickname; Nugget and Bubbly didn't like their normal selves. Once, earlier in the year, I spilled an apple juice carton on Ms. Bev's rug, underneath the upside-down world map, with Africa and South America twice as large as

America and Europe. After that, Nugget and Bubbly wanted to call me Nigerian Juiceman. That name was too long to catch on. And it wasn't me.

Ms. Bev followed Principal Big Ass into the hall. She looked at us over her shoulder before closing the door.

"See, Nugget," Bubbly said. "That's fear."

"I think I'm always afraid," Nugget said.

"I know, Nugget." Bubbly patted his back. "I know."

GRANDMA THOUGHT MS. Bev should go down the river.

"For a swim?" I asked.

"The river, Claude," she said. "Listen."

I was listening. She sat on the faded White Sox carpet next to my bed and rubbed my feet.

"You never listen, Claude," she said again. I always listened. Paul leaned against my doorjamb, arms and legs crossed. I thought about pushing him over.

"He does listen," Paul said.

"She really shouldn't put you kids through her shit," she said.

Grandma covered her mouth, apologized through her fingers. She wasn't supposed to swear around me. Through her fingers, she swore again.

I called Bubbly my bitch one day at recess. Principal Big Ass heard and called Grandma. Grandma wanted to know what the context was. Principal Big Ass told her. She was ambivalent about it. He wasn't. We had to change: no more swearing.

Paul told me to call Bubbly my sunshine.

"You kids aren't learning anything." She brought my foot up to her lips. Her lipstick felt like chalk. She had a date.

"Nugget loves bologna," I said.

"Nugget is an idiot," Paul said.

"Nugget's my friend," I said.

"And that Tiffany," Grandma said, picking at my big toenail. "That Tiffany is fast."

I shouldn't have told Grandma that Bubbly and I kissed. She called Bubbly a skank.

"I'm going to marry her," I said.

"Let's pick out a ring tonight," Paul said.

"Then you're going to marry a fast woman that will break your heart," she said. I pulled my knees to my chest.

"You're fast," I said.

Paul whistled and left. Grandma palmed my face. She left too. Her long purple dress got caught in my door. I heard a rip, her running down the steps, the front door slam. That was 8:00 p.m.

LATER, PAUL OPENED my door with an empty beer in hand.

"Let's go get that ring," he said.

Paul didn't shovel our walk, even when the snow got deep. He carried me to the salted sidewalk by my armpits. Rainbow Bar was three blocks away. Wind tossed me around. Paul dragged me along. I slipped on ice. He said sorry. The Temptations were playing over the speaker when we arrived. We both nodded at the bartender and went to the backroom.

"I love babysitting," Paul said.

Teeth was there, waiting, patient.

"I hear you want to fuck someone, Claude." Teeth stood up and kissed Paul.

"We're not swearing anymore," Paul said, an arm around Teeth's waist.

"Is that what Claude wants to do?" Teeth asked. "Do you want to fuck someone?"

"No," I said. "I just want to marry her."

"What are you going to do when you're married?" Teeth asked me.

"Go on adventures," I said.

"What are we going to do when we get married?" Teeth asked Paul.

"Go to the moon," Paul said.

"Yeah," I said. "I'd go to the moon with Bubbly."

"Why does love always start with the moon?" Teeth asked.

"Bubbly is my sunshine," I said.

Teeth crouched in front of me.

Paul didn't speak about Teeth much at home. Grandma didn't approve. She thought Teeth was a bad influence and a layabout. Grandma wanted Paul to date a nice man, for once; someone out and proud and successful. What I first knew about true love and happy relationships, I learned from Teeth and Paul in Rainbow Bar's backroom.

"What will you do for your sunshine?" Teeth asked. "Will you protect your sunshine from this cruel world? Will you guide your sunshine through any perils? Will you pay the bills?

Will you walk the dogs? Will you take out the trash? Will you hold your sunshine when there's thunder outside? Will you rock the baby to sleep? Will you drive the kids to school? Will you bury your sunshine in the most expensive coffin?"

"Yes," I said. "Of course."

"Leave him alone," Paul said to Teeth.

"Is that what you do for Paul?" I asked Teeth.

"For Paul," Teeth said, "I do anything."

Teeth's sister was in our class also. She sat three rows behind Nugget. Teeth refused to understand the law. Paul and Teeth had dated for six months. It was our secret. Most people knew. Still—Teeth was twenty years younger than Paul. He used to play professional tennis. He was tall and had a spider tattooed on his cheek.

Teeth picked me up.

Teeth spent five years in Cook County for repeated and aggressive gun possession.

Teeth put me down. Paul pushed me toward a foldout chair facing a wall. I sat like I always did and pretended not to listen.

"If you love me, Timothy," Paul said, "you'll move away."

"I can't right now," Teeth said.

"Then when?" Paul asked.

"Why do we have to leave?" Teeth asked.

"This place isn't good for us," Paul said.

"This place isn't good for anybody," Teeth said.

"Let's go to Italy," Paul said.

"I can't," Teeth said.

"Why not?" Paul asked.

"I just can't," Teeth said. "Do you understand? I just can't leave this place. What am I going to do? What place would take me? There's nothing I can do."

"We can love each other," Paul said.

"We can love each other anywhere," Teeth said. "I'll love you always."

"We can love each other in Florida," Paul said.

"I'll love you between heaven and hell," Teeth said. "I'll love you into other dimensions, into other lives."

They went on about love and leaving and staying and possibilities. Real love, I learned that night, is compromise. Teeth agreed to consider a life in Florida. Paul agreed to give Teeth some time to think about it. Teeth kissed Paul goodbye.

Teeth crouched in front of me.

"When you have your sunshine," Teeth said, "don't let your sunshine take you to Florida."

Teeth stood up and kissed Paul one more time. We left him standing at the bar.

Snow started falling when we left Rainbow Bar.

PAUL GOT A call in the morning. Teeth. Metra tracks. Flattened. A fatal accident. According to news reports, Teeth shot himself before falling down.

Paul sat at the edge of my bed until Grandma called for breakfast. He filled his glass with white wine and told me it was juice.

"Life isn't like this," Grandma said, with her hand on Paul's. "Everybody doesn't leave you."

Paul took his pancakes and wine up to his room.

GRANDMA PULLED ME to school, through the snow, in her slim wake.

Ms. Bev told us Teeth's little sister was taking time off from school. She told us to take out our math notebooks. We worked on fractions while Ms. Bev ate chicken marsala.

"Did you hear what happened?" I asked Bubbly.

"Yeah," she said. "I heard the sirens. My parents had to go to work."

Bubbly's parents wrote for the *Defender*.

"What happened?" Nugget turned around.

"Don't you live next to the Metra, Nugget?" Bubbly asked.

"Something bad, Nugget," I said.

"I'm a heavy sleeper," Nugget said. "My mom has to shake me in the morning."

We told him. His eraser dropped out of his mouth. It bounced off the tile.

"That's going to give me nightmares," he said. "I'm sad."

"You're scared," I told him.

"Thanks." He turned around and forgot his eraser.

I asked Bubbly if she wanted to marry me.

"I want to bury you?'" she asked.

My hands got slick with sweat.

"No," I said. "Marry me."

Principal Big Ass walked in.

"Claude," he said. "That's enough."

He stood at the front of the room. His ass blocked Ms. Bev.

"I'm sure Mrs. Beverley told you about what happened to Tanya's older brother," he said.

"It's Ms. Bev," Nugget said. "He exploded on the train tracks."

"Jeffrey," he said. "Do you want to spend lunch in my office?" Nugget put his head on his desk.

"I know a lot of you are close with Tanya," Principal Big Ass continued. "We arranged for the city to send a counselor. He'll be here tomorrow. I want you to go home, talk with your parents, and come prepared to discuss. That's your homework."

"My parents think a police officer tied him to the tracks because Teeth wouldn't fuck him."

"Tiffany," Principal Big Ass said, in his disappointed voice. "My office. Now."

Bubbly packed her backpack and stomped out the door without saying goodbye. I wanted to tie Principal Big Ass to the tracks.

"Fuck, shit, fuck, shit," I said.

"Very funny, Claude," he said. "Mr. Funny is getting close to detention."

He left before I could close the deal. Nugget moved to Bubbly's desk so I could help him find common denominators.

GRANDMA HAD A date in the Gold Coast with some professor; I zipped up her midnight blue dress.

"What happened to Grandpa?" I asked.

"Bad moonshine," Grandma said.

"What's moonshine?" I asked.

"Like Proud Mary in a draught," Grandma said.

"What?" I asked.

"Wildfire," Grandma said.

Paul, when he got sad, hid under Grandma's bed. From down there, he laughed.

"Where did you meet Paul?" I asked.

"Paul was an accident," Grandma said. She reached under the bed and rubbed Paul's head.

"We met in New York," she said. "After your Grandpa died."

"And fell in love?" I asked.

"No," she said. "He stole fifty dollars from me."

"Seventy," Paul said.

"Seventy," Grandma said. "He promised me seventy dollars for a photo shoot and didn't pay me."

"Grandma was hot," Paul said.

"Grandma's still hot, baby." Grandma patted her backside, patted my head, patted wrinkles around her mouth, patted her gray hair.

"I had your mom and needed a place to stay," Grandma said. "Paul let me stay at his place."

"Then Grandma made a movie and took me along for the ride." Paul slid his head back under the bed. I saw the movie once. It was horrible, black and white without direction. Grandma was beautiful; she played a queen.

"Now we're here," Grandma said. "In Chicago. Surrounded by fast little harlots."

"You're fast," I said.

She put her knee in my back and left.

I sat on her faded orange carpet and looked at the top of Paul's head. He was staring at the bottom of Grandma's box spring.

"I'm supposed to talk to you about death," I said. "For homework."

He tilted his head back and looked at me upside down.

"We should've sent you to private school," he said.

"Principal Big Ass said we have to talk about death," I said.

"Principal Big Ass likes women to pour hot wax on his nipples and call him kitty cat." Paul crawled out and stood above me.

"What?" I asked.

"Your parents abandoned you, right?" He headed for the door.

"Right," I said.

"One day Grandma and I are going to abandon you also." He had his back turned to me. "And Tiffany."

"Bubbly," I said.

"Bubbly and Nugget," he said. "And you're going to be alone."

He told me to go to sleep as he walked down the stairs. I stared at my ceiling until Grandma came home. I listened to them through my floor. Paul couldn't stop crying.

Ms. Bev introduced the person from the city. He looked like he came straight from a funeral. Principal Big Ass sat behind Ms. Bev.

"Class," Ms. Bev said over her pizza. "This is Mr. Something."

"Mr. Smithing," he said.

"Mr. Smith." She picked up her pizza and left the room.

"I am Mr. Smithing," he said again, "but you can call me Chuck."

"I'm Nugget," Nugget said.

"That's nice," Mr. Smithing said.

Bubbly wasn't there.

"Do you guys know why I'm here?" Mr. Smithing asked.

"Because death," someone shouted from the back row.

"Because we're too young to die," another voice said.

"My mom says people like you get off on violence and despair."

"I'm here to help you," Mr. Smithing said. "Let's play a game."

Mr. Smithing handed out notecards and colored pens and asked us to describe our greatest fear. After five minutes, he clapped his hands.

"Let's start here." Mr. Smithing pointed at Nugget. "What's your biggest fear?"

"I'm afraid I'll wake up and no one will be there," Nugget said.

"That does sound scary," Mr. Smithing said. "What about that scares you?"

"My mom says I have too much love in my heart," Nugget said. "She says I cry when I'm alone because my heart is too big for one person."

"Do you think your heart is too big?" Mr. Smithing asked.

"I think my heart is just the right size," Nugget said.

"I think so too," Mr. Smithing said.

Mr. Smithing focused on me.

"What are you afraid of?" Mr. Smithing asked me.

"The person I love dying," I said.

"That is scary," Mr. Smithing said.

"I know," I said.

"What is scary about that?" Mr. Smithing asked.

"I don't want to stay up all night crying," I said.

"Are you staying up all night now?" Mr. Smithing asked.

"Paul is," I said.

"Who's Paul?" Mr. Smithing asked.

"Paul was fucking Teeth," I said.

"Claude McKay Love," Principal Big Ass said. "Do you want me to call your grandmother?"

"They were in love," I said.

"They were fucking," Nugget said.

"I'm calling both of your parents," Principal Big Ass said. "My office."

We packed our bags and stomped out. Nugget rubbed his too-large heart.

NUGGET PLAYED WITH his bologna sandwich. He ripped at the crust, took it apart, smeared the mustard, licked his lips, inhaled deep. Principal Big Ass sat in his office and tried to call our families. Every couple minutes, he'd appear to let us know that he was trying again, and we were in a lot of trouble.

"Why did you swear?" I asked Nugget.

"I didn't want you to get in trouble alone," he said.

"Thanks," I said.

"Where's Bubbly?" He sucked on a bologna slice rolled into a cigar.

"I don't know," I said.

"I want to marry her," he said.

Grandma came in wearing a bathrobe and knee-high boots. She drove a knuckle into my skull. She grabbed my neck and pulled me into Principal Big Ass's office. Nugget seemed not to notice. He smiled, lips stained with mustard.

"Ms. Trueheart." Principal Big Ass tried not to stare. "Please have a seat."

"Was he swearing again?" She forced me into a chair. "We haven't been swearing."

"Yes," he said. "But I'm afraid it's much worse than that."

Grandma wasn't wearing makeup. The bags under her eyes throbbed.

"Was he kissing that little girl?" She twisted my kneecap.

"Ms. Trueheart," Principal Big Ass said, in his caring voice, "I think Claude's depressed."

Grandma's grip relaxed. Her wrinkles and bags loosened.

"Didn't his parents leave in winter? Wasn't it snowing?"

"No, fall," Grandma said, "and I should kick your fucking ass. Making me think my grandson is acting like some delinquent."

"Well, he is," Principal Big Ass said. "But that's not the point."

Principal Big Ass thought the point was loneliness and isolation. He thought I shouldn't talk with Nugget; on that count, Grandma agreed. Principal Big Ass thought Bubbly was a bad influence; on that count, Grandma agreed. He thought if things didn't change for me—he's seen countless kids like me fall through the cracks and end up dead like Teeth.

"There isn't a crack big enough to swallow him," Grandma said. "My grandson will spend his life conquering people like you."

She dragged me out. I waved at Nugget. He didn't notice. He was licking his fingers and wiping mustard off his nose.

We passed Ms. Bev outside. I waved at her. She was taking big gulps out of her soup thermos. She looked at me but didn't wave. She crammed a fistful of oyster crackers in her mouth and took another gulp.

A barrier of tightly packed, black, crystallized snow blocked us from the street. It was a bad winter. I tried to keep up with Grandma. We reached our house. She cupped my armpits and carried me to the front door. Paul nursed a hangover in the living room. He asked what was up? Grandma spanked me to my room. I sat alone on my carpet. I listened to them argue about my direction.

I SPENT THE rest of the week helping Paul build a Lego castle. Grandma found a man she could spend more than one night with. He worked in insurance, or bail bonds. Paul stopped leaving the house. Snow mountains narrowed the sidewalks. Grandma was a part-time secretary downtown. Paul freelanced for local newspapers, photographed parades and graduations. Most times, neither worked.

After that year, Bubbly's parents decided to homeschool her, and Grandma and Paul sent me to a Catholic school across the tracks.

I had to wear a mud-brown shirt and coffee-beige pants to school. The white nuns shook their heads, sucked their teeth at my wrong answers. On a Wednesday, in the bathroom, between classes, the other boys threw liquid soap at me, said my shoes were busted, said they'd kick my ass if I used the bathroom again. In the stalls, they puffed cheap weed from lunchroom apples. I was a pointless new kid: bad at sports, no jokes, no rich parents, no excellent homework to steal and copy. Grandma and Paul walked with me in the morning, tried to hold my hand, tried to kiss my cheeks, waved goodbye for too long, called my name when I didn't wave back. They did this in pajamas, hair all crazy. A few months in, one sad-eyed classmate pulled me aside at lunch. He knew how it was, having parents like that, looking messed up, smoking dope in the house, forgetting to buy groceries, forgetting to shower, smoking dope in the street. Tears filled his sad eyes. He patted my shoulder, went back to eat with his friends, left me alone, didn't speak with me again. I didn't have a chance to correct him.

I'd pass Bubbly's house on the walk back home. I'd look up at the sky if I saw her on the porch with her mother. I'd wave if she was on the porch by herself. Sometimes she'd wave back. Sometimes she'd look away and wouldn't see me. I'd try again on the walk back.

She was playing catch with her dad the last time I saw her. There was a moving truck in her driveway. I waved. Her dad looked at me, whispered something to Bubbly, and went inside. Bubbly picked up the football and bounced over.

"We're moving to Oak Park," Bubbly said. "Mom and dad got new jobs."

"I want to marry you," I said.

"I know," Bubbly said. "But your breath stinks."

"They bully me at school," I said, "because they think Paul and Grandma are scary."

"They are," Bubbly said. "And you're a baby."

I tried to kick the football but slipped and fell on the grass. Bubbly stood over me.

"My dad said Ms. Bev swam out into Lake Michigan," she said. "He said she sank to the bottom. That's why they can't find her."

Ms. Bev didn't deserve that, if that's what happened. I haven't searched for the true story. I like to imagine her on a white beach somewhere hot, drinking iced drinks, eating fresh fruit, lounging with a tanned younger man with a large heart, sleeping through the night.

I tried to stand, slipped again.

Bubbly laughed. Her dad called from the screen door. And that was it. I sat there for a moment. I got to school late. The nun made me stand facing the wall. The kids laughed at my wet butt.

A FEW MONTHS later, Grandma and the nuns had it out. Grandma thought abstinence was a pipe dream; the nuns thought Grandma was immoral, maybe evil. The nuns thought the students were too young for such improper thoughts and temptations. Grandma told the nuns to shove it.

I transferred to Crispus Attucks Middle School. Nugget went to a magnet school up north, one of those schools with a middle school and high school in a big building with big windows. He graduated valedictorian. He went to Northwestern for history, Yale for law. He moved to New York. He blogged about urban decline and America's moral decay. He organized rallies whenever the police shot an unarmed black kid. He flew back to Chicago for civil rights summits, conversations about violence and economic development. There are pictures of him online laughing with Obama. His parachute didn't open on his fortieth birthday. I went to his funeral. I couldn't find a seat.

When Nugget crosses my mind, he's blurred and brilliant, busted and smiling. I see him sucking on an eraser; I see him scared, confused. There's a lesson floating, I think, somewhere inside Nugget's everlasting spirit. When I see him, sometimes, in my dreams, it makes sense. I see him ecstatic. I see him lathering mustard on bologna. I see him small, like we remained young.

That's Nugget.

There's Nugget.

Bubbly married an accountant.

Ms. Bev is still missing.

Cookout

////////////////////////////

I DIDN'T GET better. Paul and Grandma thought I'd settle into the changes: new school, no friends, no parents, harder math problems, bullies. One night, I heard them listing my problems in the kitchen: sentimental, no backbone, adrift, unspectacular. I wanted a glass of water. I went back upstairs, parched. Of course, I cried. I cried all the time, too often. The next morning, Grandma made me watch as she swept pictures of my parents off the piano into a trash can.

"A cleanse," Grandma called it.

That was a Monday.

Each day, for the rest of the week, Grandma destroyed something poisoned with my parents' spirits.

Tuesday: she stepped on Dad's favorite Temptations records while playing the Four Tops on a boom box.

"Not the solo David Ruffin; that doesn't count," she said. "You can't expect me to—I mean, it's David Ruffin—come on."

Wednesday: she took a weed whacker to all of Mom's remaining dresses and pantsuits.

Thursday: she took me to the roller rink to meet girls, didn't care about my backward rhythm and flat feet.

Friday: she took me to the park, to make friends, for fresh air, human interaction; she took me back home when I saw an injured squirrel and cried.

Nothing worked.

Saturday: the Bulls.

I cried whenever I passed our Michael Jordan portrait in the foyer. I cried whenever I sipped from my Phil Jackson mug. I cried whenever I passed our portrait of Craig Hodges wearing a dashiki, also in the foyer, above Jordan.

The championships were over: those times were never coming back.

GRANDMA'S LIGHTER WAS gold-plated, fueled to the brim, and dangling from her fingertips over a pile of Bulls memorabilia.

She had an epiphany: gasoline.

"Go get something potent," Grandma said to Paul, who was standing next to me, there, in the backyard, underneath a crabapple tree, near a pile of tiny rotting fruit.

I was crying then, there, in the backyard. Grandma was sick of it. She had stopped consoling me. She had stopped acknowledging my runny nose and puffy eyes. When I cried before bed, she didn't come running down the hall with her robe open.

Paul sprinted out of the house with a clear jug half-filled with clear, sloshing liquid.

"What's that?" Grandma asked, taking her eyes off me.

"Burn through diamonds," Paul said, took a swig from the jug before handing it to Grandma.

"Wait," I said.

Grandma and Paul looked me over, paused, stopped pouring the clear liquid on a cardboard Dennis Rodman.

"Baby," Grandma said.

"Fire purifies," Paul said.

"We can't blame the Bulls," I said. "They didn't do anything wrong."

I pulled my Horace Grant T-shirt from the pile and went upstairs.

"Thank God," I heard Grandma say behind me.

"Goddamn," I heard Paul say. "Alright. He's alright."

In the basement, that night, I came across Grandma dancing with cardboard Dennis Rodman, leading him across the unfinished floor, twirling, dipping, listening to David Ruffin sing about Georgia and rain. She didn't see me then, there, halfway down the stairs. She was wearing a commemorative sweatshirt from the first three-peat. I saw her smiling, eyes closed, far away. That smile I hadn't seen before. It was pure and light. For me, she was willing to burn her happiness. For her, I stopped crying.

ON SUNDAY, WHEN Grandma noticed my dry eyes and lifted chin at breakfast, she stood, walked around the table, kissed my forehead, didn't say anything, walked back to her Belgian waffle.

"Alright," Paul said. "Goddamn. Alright."

Jonah and the Dunk

THE JULY BEFORE I started eighth grade, Paul had this scare. A blemish on an X-ray. After tests and hours of chain-smoking—nothing serious, just an aberration. Paul chain-smoked whenever he felt helpless. Paul chain-smoked in celebration, steak on his plate, whiskey at his goblet's brim.

"If I'm going to die," Paul said, "I'm swinging. Happy."

The doctors wanted him to change. Paul thought change meant melding into society, following, not leading. Grandma called him ridiculous. It was just steak, cigarettes, and hard liquor, not the right to vote.

"If I'm going to die," Paul said, cutting a bite-size triangle out of a New York strip, "I'm going to do it proud."

Jonah moved in up the street a month later.

Jonah's dad was a cop. His mom decorated houses up in Lincoln Park, up on the North Side. Jonah dressed like he was a pro. He was over six feet. I hadn't hit puberty yet. He dribbled up and down the block, between his legs, behind his back. I wanted his Nike sweatpants and Jordan tank tops. Paul only bought me Adidas. He thought kids got killed over Nikes and Jordans. Jonah moved like liquid.

"So, Jonah," Paul asked when Grandma invited the new neighbors over, "you ball like the devil?"

"Yes, sir," Jonah said.

"What's that supposed to mean?" Jonah's dad asked.

"Bad," Paul said. "You know, bad as hell."

"Oh," Jonah's mom said.

"What about you?" Jonah's dad asked me.

"What?" I asked back.

"You ball?" Jonah's dad asked me.

"Claude's too angelic," Paul said.

"That's wonderful," Jonah's mom said to me.

"Where did you play?" Jonah's dad asked Paul.

"Paul can't shoot dead fish," Grandma said from the kitchen.

"I learned in a cage," Paul said.

"What?" I asked everybody.

"The cage up the street?" Jonah's dad asked Paul.

"Up from the Rucker," Paul said, leaned back, rubbed his belly.

"Wait," Jonah's dad said, held up his arms.

"Hold up," Jonah's mom said.

"What's a cage?" I asked everybody, again.

"You're not from Chicago?" Jonah's mom asked Paul.

"New York is basketball," Paul said.

"New York," Jonah's dad said to his hands.

"Mecca," Paul said.

"You're from New York?" Jonah's dad asked.

"You're asking my son about basketball," Jonah's mom said.

"Who do you think you are?" Jonah's dad asked.

"Where do you get off?" Jonah's mom asked.

"I played against Tim Hardaway," Jonah's dad said.

"Me too," Jonah's mom said. "He's my little cousin."

"Doc Rivers," Jonah's dad said. "Cazzie Russell gave me his shoes."

"Juwan Howard drove me to school every morning," Jonah's mom said.

"Michael Jordan was born in Brooklyn," Paul said.

"Nate Archibald!" Grandma yelled from the kitchen.

"Ben Wilson is a saint!" Jonah's dad yelled.

"Isiah Thomas!" Jonah's mom yelled.

"Lew Alcindor!" Grandma yelled.

They yelled names at each other until Grandma served the pasta. They yelled with forks in their mouths, spit marinara across the table. Jonah and I sat there, exchanged apologetic looks. When Grandma put down her apple pie, Jonah's mom gave up.

"Jonah," Jonah's mom said. "We're leaving."

"Jonah," Jonah's dad said. "Scottie Pippen is better than Patrick Ewing."

"Madison Square Garden!" Grandma yelled as they drove away.

Under his breath, while we cleaned the dishes, Paul muttered. "Willis Reed, Willis Reed, Willis Reed, Willis Reed."

AFTER MIDNIGHT, SOMEONE threw rocks at my window. It was Jonah.

"Let's hoop tomorrow," Jonah said.

"I'm not good," I said.

"It's just hooping," Jonah said.

"Okay," I said. "Cool."

I LEARNED, IN the morning, about cages and courts. Paul and Grandma sat me down before school.

There weren't many cages in Chicago. Courts were open air and surrounded by trees. The high schoolers played on Lake Shore Drive, closer to the beach, where the girls hung out, on a sand-dusted court. A standard cage had chain link fencing all around the court, painted green or black. Fencing in the players—that was a New York thing. Grandma thought cages made us look like animals. Paul thought cages treated basketball like a precious act, something to protect from the dangerous world.

Jackson Park had a cage next to the golf course. We had the cage to ourselves. Jonah brought his five-year-old brother. Paul sat on the concrete with a beer. He patted the ground for Jonah's little brother to take a seat.

The rims were soft and forgiving. Any shot worth anything went in. Jonah's imperfect shots would spin, roll, and fall. His perfect shots would crack the net like a whip. I tried fancy layups that didn't come close. Paul told me to stop acting like some Rucker Park disciple. Just feed the devil the ball, he told me. Jonah's little brother nodded in agreement. So I did. I passed the ball to Jonah. He cared for it. He never looked at it. His eyes only showed concern the rare times he mishandled it, let it roll away, let it bounce above his waist. He was noble and righteous. He was spectacular.

As the sun went down, Jonah told his little brother to stand in front of the basket. He told me to throw the ball in the air.

"When?" I asked.

"You'll know," he said, and walked to half court. He turned around and started running. When he got to the three-point line, he looked at me.

"Now!" Paul yelled.

"Now!" Jonah's little brother yelled.

"Now, Claude, now!" Paul yelled again.

"Now!" I yelled, and tossed.

Jonah took off from the free-throw line. He spread his legs and caught the ball with one hand. He cleared his little brother by a foot. It looked like he would fly out of the cage and land somewhere in Ohio. He was a low-flying jet in the dusk. He returned to earth like a breaching whale. My legs quivered. Paul ran over and hugged him. His little brother held on to his waist.

"See that, Claude?" Paul asked. "That's how sex feels.

"My God, son," Paul said to Jonah. "You are a religion."

The sun went down. We walked back in reverie. I noticed beauty in everything: the warped chain-link fence, the tags on the bus-stop advertisements, the glimmer from broken glass in the gutter, the breeze carrying sewer smells. We left the brothers on Jonah's doorstep.

In our living room, Paul went face first into the couch.

"If that boy ever stops balling," Paul said into a cushion, "the world will end."

Grandma looked up from her book and asked what happened. I told her Paul had been converted.

IN THE KITCHEN, over breakfast, Paul vowed to quit smoking. Cigarettes were too expensive.

"And they're poison," Grandma said.

"And they turn us into zombies," Paul agreed.

"And they cost too damn much," Grandma said.

"And I can't breathe," Paul said.

"A glass of wine," Grandma said.

"That's all I need," Paul agreed.

"Quitting something is an important exercise in self discovery," Grandma said.

"I will find myself," Paul said.

"And Claude," Grandma said.

"And Claude," Paul said.

They wanted a response from me.

"Jonah knows who he is," I said. "I want to know who I am."

Jonah showed up while I was scraping eggs into the garbage can.

For the first time, he looked human. His eyes were glazed and baggy. His face was dull and unglowing.

"I killed him," Jonah said.

He wasn't covered in blood. He wasn't holding a weapon. His clothes were crusted around his collar and armpits.

"Jonah," Grandma said. "What are you talking about?"

"He's dead." Jonah sat on the table. His feet touched the floor. His little brother had collapsed at breakfast. His parents took him to the emergency room. They told Jonah to wait at our house for the phone call. We were the only option. They didn't have any other friends.

"How could you be responsible?" Grandma asked.

"He told me I was his favorite big brother," Jonah said. "Then he collapsed."

"It's okay, son," Paul said. "These things happen."

At that moment, I wished I knew Jonah better. I wanted to know if he could kill his admirers.

"Your brother is not dead," Grandma said.

Jonah's parents showed up around lunch. His brother wasn't dead. Just in a coma. Paul burned cheese sandwiches on the stove. Grandma stroked Jonah's head.

I didn't see Jonah for three weeks. I waited for him at the cage with Paul. I walked past his house. No one was there during the day. At night, the lights were out.

Then school started. Jonah walked in five minutes late, sat next to me, didn't fit in his seat right, asked if I wanted to eat lunch with him. I was too surprised to say yes. I nodded. He nodded.

George Bones and the rest of the basketball team clapped their trays onto our table.

"I hear your dunks vaporize people," George Bones said.

I stood up. Jonah pulled me down by my bicep.

George Bones could dribble two basketballs at a time, blindfolded.

"I can't dunk," Jonah said. He stared at George Bones; George Bones blinked first.

"You should play with us after school," George Bones said. "Coach lets us use the gym."

He wouldn't look at Jonah. Jonah looked right through him.

"Claude can't come," George Bones continued. "He has to go fuck his grandma."

I caressed my fork. They laughed and walked away.

When the team left, Coach Harper sat down.

"Don't listen to them, Claude," he said, looking over Jonah. "You might make the team this year. We need someone to clean up after practice."

Coach Harper chewed five pieces of gum at a time. Grandma thought he was an asshole. Dad's Coach, the coach I knew well, thought Coach Harper didn't belong in the basketball universe.

"So." He smacked at Jonah. "You can dunk?"

"No," Jonah said.

"Not what I hear," Coach Harper said.

Jonah stood up. I did too.

"Wait, wait," Coach Harper said. "You know who I am, right?"

"Yes," I said.

"Shut up, Claude," Coach Harper said.

"Yes," Jonah said.

"I can destroy you," Coach Harper said.

I didn't know what he was talking about. Jonah didn't care. I cared. I was terrified.

"How will you destroy us?" I asked.

"No one cares about you, Claude," Coach Harper said to Jonah. His gum blob fell on the table. He picked it up, put it back in, and chewed like crazy.

"If Claude plays," Jonah said, "I'll play."

"He can carry your shoes," Coach Harper said to Jonah.

"I can do that," I said.

"We have good chemistry," Jonah said.

"We do?" I asked Jonah.

"Just come to the gym after school," Coach Harper said

"Do we have a deal?" Jonah asked.

"If you beat George Bones," Coach Harper said, "Claude can start at point guard."

"Really?" I asked Coach Harper.

"With you," Coach Harper said to Jonah, "we only need four players anyway."

"After school," Jonah said.

"After school," I said.

"After school," Coach Harper said.

Coach Harper left.

"You shouldn't be so weak all the time," Jonah said to me.

GEORGE BONES AND the other guys were shooting around when Jonah and I walked in. They had on Jordans, Kobes, and LeBrons. Jonah wore jeans and boots. Coach Harper blew his whistle. He told everyone to sit in the bleachers, except Jonah and George Bones. He rolled Jonah a ball.

"You need anything, Jonah?" Coach Harper asked. "A Go-Gurt? Some Gatorade? A pair of Nikes?"

"Maybe a doctor," George Bones said.

"Alrighty then." Coach Harper tried to blow his whistle, but gum blocked it. The sound came out wet. "George, you start. First to twenty-one. Twos and threes. Keeps. Let's ball."

George Bones had possession of the ball for two full dribbles. Then Jonah stole it and hit seven threes in a row, and we left.

"Claude plays," Jonah said from the doorway.

PAUL SAW JONAH'S hand in anything miraculous. Paul claimed Jonah was behind the winning lottery ticket for Ms. Dunewell, the young widow from Seventy-Second Street. He led me into his room. He presented his corkboard. It was like something from a movie about insanity. Thin slips of newspaper were thumbtacked in a chaotic array.

FIREMEN ARRIVE JUST IN TIME TO SAVE KITTENS.

MOTHER OF THREE BARELY ESCAPES SINKING CAR.

DEPUTY MAYOR INDICTED.

REDBELTERS STASH HOUSE RAIDED.

CRIME RATES AT RECORD LOW.

"You see what this boy is doing?" Paul beamed.

It was almost Halloween. The season was a month away. A story about five teenagers, former drug dealers, finding God and becoming altruistic was displayed in the middle of Paul's madness.

"But I thought Jonah was the devil?" I asked.

"The devil works in mysterious ways." Paul lay on his bed, facing the heavens.

"Leave Claude alone," Grandma called as she walked past. "Just because you're crazy doesn't mean he has to be."

Paul was still lying there when I left for the cage.

Of course I already knew Jonah was a savior. I didn't need Paul to tell me that. The world was kinder with Jonah in it, sweeter, benevolent, unfamiliar. Jonah awoke faith in me. His spirit guided mine.

GEORGE BONES WAS standing under the hoop when I showed up at the cage. No one else was there. George Bones usually balled on Lake Shore Drive, putting on a show for the girls.

"I've been practicing," George Bones said. "Let's play."

"I'm just gonna wait for Jonah." He could tell I wanted to run.

"Come on." He took a step closer. I took a step back. He took a step closer. I bumped into the chain-link.

"Let's practice."

He threw the ball at my chest. I dropped it. It rolled back to him. He threw it like a football. It hit my head. I slid to the ground.

"Jonah's gonna kick your ass," I said.

I didn't see him move. Somehow, he knocked me down. He stood over me.

"What did you say?"

I said, "Jonah's gonna vaporize you."

He took my head between his palms and drove his knee into my face.

I thought I saw a flash of light. I thought a beam took George Bones and lifted him off the ground. There was heat all around me. Heat and light pulsing down my spine. I knew Jonah would come. I thought I saw him lift George Bones over his head. I thought I saw him throw George Bones like a paper bag filled with quarters. I thought I heard George Bones explode against the concrete.

I WOKE UP in the hospital. My eyes were swollen shut. I heard Coach Harper.

"Don't you fucking scream, Claude," he said.

"Why would I scream?" I asked. "Where am I?"

"You're in hell," he said close to my ear. "Don't you say a fucking word."

I smelled a pile of mint green.

"You say anything," he sounded farther away, "and I'll destroy you."

"How will you destroy me?" I asked. But he was gone. I asked again.

"What the hell are you talking about," Grandma's voice was over me. "Did they give you drugs? Nurse. Did you give him drugs?"

"The voice," I said. "The voice said it was going to destroy me."

"Nurse!" Grandma yelled down the hall.

A nurse hurried in, wiped smudged frosting from her cheeks and full mouth.

"Was someone in here with my grandson?" Grandma asked.

The nurse swallowed.

"It's Raven's birthday," the nurse said. "We were eating cupcakes. She's thirty. Her father came down from Waukegan."

"Did you give him drugs?" Grandma asked.

"Why would I do a thing like that?" The nurse walked out the door.

Grandma rubbed my forehead.

"Don't worry," Grandma said. "You're just going a little crazy."

I SPENT TWO days in the hospital with two broken ribs, a broken nose, a concussion, and a scuffed-up face. I was discharged on Halloween. Little monsters banged on our windshield when Grandma pulled up.

Mothers screamed for their children to come on, that house doesn't have any candy, move it, dark's coming.

"I'm going to kill Paul," Grandma said as she led me up to our porch.

Paul was dressed like a cross between Madonna and Diana Ross. He held empty bottles of vodka in each hand. He only drank vodka when he ran out of cigarettes and the world was closing in on him. He was supposed to go to a party up north. He was supposed to leave a bowl of candy on the porch.

"Hell has risen on our doorstep." Paul clanked his bottles together. "The trumpet sounds and our chariot awaits."

"Claude"—Grandma led Paul into the kitchen—"go to your room."

My vision was blurred still. I tripped four times going up the stairs. Jonah was on my bed.

He moved to the floor.

His brother woke up the day George Bones put me in the hospital. He'd heard I was coming home. He'd knocked on my front door and asked Paul if he could wait for me.

Seven people were shot when I was away. The neighborhood was back to normal. The miraculous disappeared. Ms. Germaine, from Seventieth Street, had a pistol stuck into her stomach for her Social Security check. Downstairs, Paul yelled about rising dead, ash falling like snow from swollen black clouds, parking tickets, forever-constant meteor showers—End Times.

"Paul begged me to kill him," Jonah said.

"Oh," I said. "He's not well."

"Sorry," Jonah said.

"About what?" I asked.

"Not sure," Jonah said.

He got up and left. I started to follow him. Then I got dizzy and had to lie back down.

I heard Grandma say "Hey, Jonah" and "Goodbye, Jonah."

I heard the front door slam.

I heard Paul make belated attempts at redemption.

I heard him scream for mercy and forgiveness.

PAUL SWORE OFF breakfast liquor. Grandma refused to cook any meal for him. He sopped up our bacon grease with stale bread.

"I'd rather die than live under that devil's thumb," Paul said, still drunk.

"Stop this nonsense," Grandma said over her full plate.

"What devil?" I asked.

"That Jonah," Paul said.

"He's just a boy," Grandma said.

"He has *power*," Paul said.

"Enough," Grandma said.

"He just balls," I said.

"Look what happened when he stopped," Paul said.

He pointed a trembling fist toward my still-bruised face.

"Paul." Grandma jabbed him with his fork. "That's enough."

"That devil might ball," Paul continued.

I smelled fear and booze.

"You scared Jonah," Grandma said to Paul.

She turned to me.

"Was it good seeing him, Claude?" she asked.

"Yeah," I said.

"Are you going to see him today?" she asked.

"Of course," I lied.

COACH HARPER AND my principal came over around lunch. They wanted to know if I remembered who attacked me. When nobody was looking, Coach Harper ran his index finger across his throat.

"I'll wait in here with little Claudey," he said when the other adults went to grab sodas from the kitchen.

"This is all I have, Claude," Coach Harper said.

He picked up a flower vase next to his chair. He put the vase down. He massaged the tulip bulbs. He studied the flower vase as he talked to me.

"If you tell them the truth," Coach Harper said, "they'll kick George Bones off the team."

I didn't know what to say to him. I didn't want to say something wrong. There was something unmistakable and unstable in his eyes.

"I'm all alone in this world," Coach Harper said. "If they kick George Bones off the team, I won't have anything."

"You'll have Jonah," I said. "We all have Jonah."

"Michael needed Scottie," Coach Harper said. "Jonah needs George if we're going to win the city championship."

He picked up the vase again. He put it down when the adults came back in.

"Now, Claude," my principal said, "I hear George Bones might have had something to do with this."

"Yeah," I said. "He did it. He did all of it. It was all him."

Fuck George Bones, I thought. Fuck Coach Harper and his ruined world.

Coach Harper picked up the flower vase and threw it at my head. He missed. He lunged at me. Grandma stuck a foot into his knee and dropped him.

"Can I go back to bed?" I asked while the adults held Coach Harper on the floor. I went upstairs.

"You ruined me!" Coach Harper yelled, stood up.

"You ruined me." Coach Harper cried, bent down.

George Bones was kicked out of school. Coach Harper was fired and ordered to counseling.

That Sunday, when Jonah and his parents came over for dinner, a bee landed on my neck. I didn't feel it. One sting would've put me in intensive care. Jonah brushed it off, and it stung his hand.

His parents were over to talk about moving. They wanted Jonah to say goodbye.

"This place is fucked up," Jonah's mom said, without hesitation.

"We're moving downstate," Jonah's dad said. "Close to Missouri."

Paul looked relieved. He lit a cigarette and smoked slowly.

"That's nice," Grandma said. "That's a good thing to do."

"That's nice," I said.

"All this craziness," Jonah's mom said. "This isn't good for raising kids."

Jonah stood over the sink, his back to us, soaking his bee sting in warm water. We looked at his back. We wanted him to say something. He didn't. He stood in his Nike gear and considered his wound. Next morning, they were gone.

JONAH STILL LIVES downstate. He doesn't play basketball. His parents got divorced. Jonah won't even visit South Shore.

A few years ago, his brother died in his sleep from an unknown disease.

I wonder if Jonah knows it wasn't his fault.

I wonder if he sees benevolence in his shadow.

Sixty-Seventh Street

GRANDMA TOOK THE swing beside me and matched my lazy rhythm. After Jonah left, I started running away. Not far; just up the block, a few blocks over, the small park on Sixty-Seventh.

"What's wrong with you and this game?" Paul would ask each time he retrieved me. Sometimes, Grandma came for me.

Once, Grandma hung with me for a little bit, swayed with me, kicked off her sandals.

"Say the word, and we'll move to Hawaii," Grandma said to me.

Silence was my other new impulse.

"Well, just listen then," Grandma said.

She put her hand on my back, pushed me gentle and slow.

"Those kids standing around that bus stop aren't going anywhere. You know what they're doing? They're not waiting for the bus. You know who those kids are? They're Redbelters, those boys and girls. Don't look too long, just glance. You know what they're doing? Those kids, boys and girls, dealing drugs. I knew them when they were you: young and sad at the world. I knew their fathers and mothers, most of them. They're smart like you. Smart enough to do basic math, smart enough to know when someone's trying to kill or fool them. That's smarter than a lot of people in this world. Still, society doesn't want them to go anywhere. Those kids aren't taking the bus. They're going to stand all day; then, they're going to stand all night. They're going to stand until dust settles on their exposed skeletons. Do you know what I mean?"

I didn't.

"I failed with your mother," Grandma continued. "The universe failed your father. I'm not going to lose you. You got something special deep in there. We don't know what it is yet. We'll find it. Don't worry. We'll find it. I've ruined too many fixable things in my life, and I'm not that old. There's hope for us yet—goddamn it, baby, I love you."

We watched the buses go by. An undercover screeched onto the sidewalk, and those Redbelters scattered.

That night I dreamed my room was a spaceship. I was a skeleton, and my ceiling fan swirled mini dust tornadoes around my bed and eyeballs. Those Redbelters were writing scriptures on my wall with pens. At least, that's what they said they were writing. Scriptures? Scriptures? I kept asking. It was all equations I didn't understand, written in the shape of a colonnade. They finished and asked me to read it back to them, starting

with the end. The end, I saw, was a chain of interconnected cir-
cles swirling around a burning building. I tried to speak, and
they all turned into skeletons, like me. Then, we all turned to
dust. We died like that; just like that.

Janice and the Redbelters

//

CHILL'S SMOKEHOUSE WAS a front. The Redbelters handed out flyers in the parking lot after school. Everyone got one. The flyers promised half-off the lunch special.

"We got fries," a large man in sunglasses told us from behind the counter. It was November and cloudy. He wore a camouflage tank top with a blue whale printed across the stomach. We tucked the fries deep in our backpacks.

That was my freshman year in high school. That was the year Chicago Public Schools lunches were deemed subhealthy. Fries were the first to go.

The next day, we hustled over.

Their marquee advertised ribs, pizza, and gyros. They didn't even have a soda machine, fryer, or oven. Fries were the lunch special. They microwaved them by the pound. Mine were cold and soggy. A bearded linebacker passed out paper plates covered in ketchup, for dipping.

"Y'all got mustard?" someone asked.

"Coming soon," the linebacker said.

Everything was coming soon. Like chairs and tables. Sticky brown and yellow stains dotted the linoleum floor. A door slammed behind the counter.

And Big Columbus appeared.

We knew we had made a mistake. Big Columbus sold drugs and guns to kids and teenagers. Big Columbus was head of the Redbelters.

"How y'all doing today?" Big Columbus asked. Someone raised a hand. Big Columbus called on him.

"I have to go home," the person said. The bearded linebacker blocked the entrance. Big Columbus ignored him.

"Who here wants to save South Shore?" Big Columbus asked.

No one answered.

"Who here wants to get rich?"

He stood up on the counter.

"Who here knows who I am?"

Everybody nodded.

"Good," Big Columbus said. "If any of you get sick of being chess pieces and want to be soldiers in the fight for sovereignty, you know where I am."

Big Columbus hopped down. The bearded linebacker moved from the door. The street outside was littered with flyers, paper plates, and fries. Ketchup splattered the sidewalk.

. . .

GRANDMA WANTED TO put Big Columbus in a headlock.

"I knew that boy when he was in diapers," Grandma said.

"How?" I asked.

"Don't worry," Grandma said.

"He said he wants to save South Shore," I said.

"Those Redbelters think they're Black Panthers," Grandma said.

"We were the struggle," Paul said.

"You were a Girl Scout," Grandma said to Paul. Paul took his pasta and went upstairs.

"They gave us fries," I said.

"They were probably microwaved," Grandma said. "And they probably didn't have any mustard."

She slapped her palms against her head.

"Don't be stupid," Grandma said to me. "If you're stupid I'm going to drop-kick you."

She kissed my eyebrow, grabbed her coat, gave Paul a gentle slap, and ran out the front door. Paul reentered the kitchen. He was holding a framed picture.

"This look like a Girl Scout to you?" Paul asked, shoved the picture in my face.

I'd seen pictures like that during Black History Month. Young Paul stood behind a man screaming over a podium. Everybody had fists raised. Most of them were wearing sunglasses and Afros. Paul was slim, muscular, smiling. He was smiling wide. He wasn't wearing glasses. His smiling eyes shone under his space-black shrublike hair.

"That's power."

He leaned back in his chair and put his hands on his belly.

"That looks like Fred Hampton," I said.

"It is Brother Fred," Paul said. "Brother Fred would make Big Columbus shine his shoes."

"They killed Fred Hampton in his sleep," I said.

"That's not his fault," Paul said.

"Whose fault is it?" I asked.

"Whenever we come together," Paul said, "they want to break us apart."

"Who's 'we'?" I asked.

"Us," Paul said.

"Who's 'they'?" I asked.

"Everybody that isn't us," Paul said.

"Why didn't they kill you?" I said.

"I'm unkillable," Paul said.

He yanked the picture out of my hand and went into the living room.

OVER THE NEXT several weeks kids stopped showing up to class. Chin, a freshman fourth-string running back, thought working for Big Columbus was safer than sprinting full speed into an immovable pile of lineman. Travis left because *Gone with the Wind* ruined his appetite for reading. Last winter, Mary Dobson had given her baby to relatives in Ohio; now, she wanted to send money. And so on. Freshman, sophomores, juniors, and seniors. They were all making money. Principal Carmichael was worried. He had principaled through the Stones and GDs. Those gangs had imploded. That took years though, generations. Principal Carmichael didn't feel like waiting for the Redbelters to self-destruct. He was old and scared and ready to make history. He called a lunchtime assembly.

We shuffled into the auditorium. I sat in the back, behind band kids and the science club.

"There is a disease among us." Principal Carmichael whispered into the microphone, for gravitas. "Let's talk about a cure."

Vice-Principal Mac yelled for him to speak up.

"We can't hear you, preacher," he yelled. Word was Vice-Principal Mac used to run guns from Indiana and sell them to Latin Kings. When we read about British sympathizers during the American Revolution, I pictured Vice-Principal Mac and his big earrings. Principal Carmichael turned the mic volume up but spoke softer.

"How many of you are scared?" Principal Carmichael asked.

The rows in front of me raised their arms.

"So here's what we're going to do," he continued.

Double doors slammed. A pigtailed girl I recognized from lunch came down the row.

"Ms. Camden, please take a seat," Principal Carmichael said in his strict voice. Then he kept whispering.

"You're Claude, right?" she asked.

"Yes," I said. Her pink T-shirt hung past her knees. Her baggy sweatpants bunched around her chunky white shoes. Her face was sharp and movielike, stunning. She smelled musty and real.

"I'm Janice," Janice said.

"I'm Claude," I said.

"I know that," Janice said.

I had nothing else to say. Janice shifted in her seat, pulled her knees up to her chin, into her T-shirt. Her head atop a pink blob.

"What is this anyway?" Janice asked.

"An assembly," I said.

"I know that," Janice said.

"I'm sorry," I said.

"You're nicer than I thought," Janice said.

"What do you mean?" I asked.

"People talk about you," Janice said.

"I know," I said.

"They say you have no friends," Janice said.

"I have friends," I said.

"They say you're going to shoot up the school," Janice said.

"I have friends," I said.

"Really?" Janice asked.

"Everyone has friends," I said.

"I don't," Janice said.

I didn't know what to say. Until then, as we had talked, I had kept my head forward, spoke sideways. Now, I looked at her, stared. She kept her head, balanced on her blob, angled down.

"Like who?" Janice asked.

"Paul," I said.

"Paul Newson?" Janice asked. "He plays baseball; he's not your friend."

"Not that Paul," I said.

"Which Paul?" Janice asked.

"You don't know him," I said.

"It's okay," Janice said.

"I'm serious," I said.

"I don't have any friends either," Janice said. "People talk about me too."

I often sat alone, a little on edge; I was used to empty seats on my left and right. Janice, in her blob, pumped warmth into my side, calmed me. Our heads were close, tilted. Adrenaline and blood pounded my eardrums. My brain rattled, flooded with warm memories, recalled love, floating sensations. I closed my eyes. Bubbly. Nugget. Jonah. All those far away people sat inside me, waved, wished me well. Most nights, outside my bedroom window, all that love felt far away, impossible to see and feel.

"Are you okay?" Janice asked.

I opened my eyes.

"No," I said. "Yes. Yes. Yes. I meant yes."

Principal Carmichael reminded us that police officers are our friends and informants aren't snitches.

"Your grandma came to my house yesterday," Janice said.

"She's going around the neighborhood," I said.

"She's a little wild," Janice said

"I'm sorry," I said. "She's worried about the future."

"I like it," Janice said. "She screamed a little."

"I'm sorry," I said again.

"They want to organize a march," Janice said.

"I'm so sorry," I said.

"They want to take back the streets," Janice said.

Principal Carmichael invited Officer Baggs onto the stage. Officer Baggs had been indicted on bribery charges the previous summer.

"My cousins want to do it," Janice said. "They're talking about getting a shotgun and two pistols for the house."

"You live with your cousins?" I asked.

"You live with your grandma?" Janice asked.

We both nodded.

Officer Baggs said da gangs are bad and ruin lives. He said da kids dat join da gangs were going to end up in da jail or da cemahtery.

"My parents moved to Missouri," I said.

"My parents died on vacation," Janice said.

She looked at me. I looked at the stage. Officer Baggs was setting up a poster board like the assembly was a science fair. He pointed to a picture I couldn't see. Janice, still, looked at me.

"When you squint," Janice said, "you look like you're going to cry."

"Sorry," I said.

"You're still cute," Janice said.

I choked on nothing, felt my heart trip a few times. Janice had slipped out of her pink blob. I didn't realize. She was a full person again, leaned back, feet on the ground. I wanted to respond, say she was cute too. I wanted to say that even as a blob, she was cute. I wanted to call her beautiful.

I stammered into her face, spit some, choked on nothing, coughed, and spit some more.

Janice smiled at me, pulled her pink shirt over her nose, muffled her laughter.

Officer Baggs left the stage.

"Be safe," Principal Carmichael said. "Take control of your future."

Janice regained composure.

"See you tonight," Janice said.

"What?" I asked.

She left me choking.

JANICE AND HER aunt and uncle, Jimmy and Annette, came over for dinner. Grandma ordered pizza. She put on a burgundy pantsuit. We brought extra chairs into the living room. Grandma was expecting twenty people. There were five pizzas for the six of us.

"This is it?" Paul came in late with a beer.

"This is Paul," Grandma said.

"Good to meet you, Paul," Jimmy said. His arms were longer than what looked natural. His chest looked sunken in.

"It's a pleasure, Paul and Catherine," Annette said. Her pigtails were the same as Janice's—except hers were gray.

"Please," Grandma said. "Call me Grandma."

I asked if I could go to my room. Grandma said I should take Janice. Janice smiled at me and we went upstairs. I took a pizza for us.

"So this is your room?" Janice asked as she opened my closet and started fingering my shirts.

"Those are old," I said. "The new stuff is in my drawers."

I opened the pizza box. Janice made me dizzy. I realized I'd taken the anchovy. The room stank like fish. I had to eat something.

"The new stuff looks like the old stuff," Janice said, shuffling through my dresser.

"How did your parents die?" I asked, and took another bite.

"Hippo attack," Janice said.

"That's tragic," I said.

She moved to my bed and watched me rock in my chair.

"Actually they were kidnapped in Venezuela and sold into sex slavery." She fell backward and looked at me sideways.

"I'm sorry to hear that," I said.

"Seriously, they were both hit on the head with coconuts in Jamaica, at the same time, but under different trees." She stood up again and walked over to me.

"That's tragic," I said.

Then she kissed me.

I remembered Bubbly telling me that my breath stank.

"I'm sorry about the pizza," I said.

"I like anchovies," Janice said.

"I'm sorry about your parents," I said.

"You'll believe anything, won't you?" Janice asked.

I nodded and she kissed me again. She pulled away again.

"How did your parents die?" Janice asked.

"They didn't," I said. "They're in Missouri."

"I thought you were lying," Janice said.

She kept her lips away from me.

"Why would you think that?" I asked.

"I don't know how you work," Janice said.

"They left when I was five," I said.

"Mine got flattened by a semi driving to Idaho in the rain," Janice said. "The driver was on methamphetamines."

"How did they know he was on methamphetamines?" I asked.

"He did the same thing to three other cars," Janice said. "It was on the news. Don't you watch the news?"

Then Janice unzipped her pants and unzipped mine. She climbed on top of me. Dawn, chemistry, physics, melding; rush, fire, an eclipse between us. Holding Janice like that— never again would I feel that close to someone. And I knew she wanted me to hold her. Someone wanting me like that—I didn't know what to think about it. Unlike anything else. I felt Janice through me. Those thirty seconds felt like two lifetimes. She climbed off me.

Something broke downstairs. Jimmy screamed Janice's name.

"Let's eat together tomorrow," Janice said.

She checked herself in the mirror. Jimmy screamed again. Janice looked over her shoulder and puckered her lips at me. She hurried out my door and down the stairs. I looked down at my exposed lap.

I zipped up my pants when I heard Grandma's heels clicking. She threw open my door. Her eyes were bulging.

"Does no one else get it?" Grandma asked my ceiling.

She stepped into the room. Her body moved in rigid and furious steps.

She took the pizza, took a step back, stopped. She sniffed. She shot me a glance and went to her room.

Downstairs, Paul swept broken glass into a paper plate. Boxes of pizza looked untouched.

I asked what happened. He sat down on the carpet and started picking up tiny shards with his fingers.

"Typical stuff," Paul said. "Violence against nonviolence."

He rubbed the carpet and then took a swig from a wine bottle. He swore under his breath when glass stuck to his palm.

"What happened?" I asked again.

"They think they're better than us," Paul said. "They don't think Grandma should lead the march."

"Here," I said. "What happened here?"

"Grandma tried to strangle her," Paul said.

"Why?" I asked.

"This thing goes back decades," Paul said.

"What thing?" I asked.

"I've lost friendships over this," Paul said.

"Over what?" I asked.

"You know," Paul said. "The struggle. The plight. This shit." He sat next to me on the couch. We stared at the pizza.

"Janice is cute," Paul said.

"We had sex," I said.

"That's not funny, Claude," Paul said. "You won't get any woman talking like that."

A FEW MONTHS later, Janice invited me over for a Bears game. Grandma's march didn't work. She'd wanted to organize a militia. Jimmy and Annette organized a different march for Martin Luther King Jr. Day. Their march would include spirituals and candles.

Each night, Grandma went to sleep angry. The house was filled with stomping and slamming doors. Paul was her only supporter, but Paul spent all his time drinking.

Grandma and Paul were getting ready for church while I was getting ready for Janice. Paul shot his remaining martini down his throat and handed me an empty glass.

"You should come with us," Grandma said while putting on her heels, her hand on Paul's shoulder for balance.

"I really love Janice," I said.

"You don't know anything," Paul said.

"You think no one matters but yourself," Grandma said.

"That's going to be the end of you and mankind," Paul said.

I left. I got to Janice's right before kickoff.

"Jimmy," Annette yelled upstairs. "Claude's here."

Annette said Janice was walking the dogs and would be back shortly. She waved me into the living room. Jimmy came running down in a Walter Payton jersey. The three of us squeezed onto the couch and put the game on mute.

"You look like a good kid," Jimmy said. "How did that happen?"

"Jimmy," Annette said. "That's not fair."

"What?" Jimmy asked. "Isn't it fair to say Claude could have turned out terrible?"

I sat between them. They were talking over my head. I didn't realize how tall they were, how small I was.

"Jimmy," Annette said, "Claude's had a rough life."

"He's impressive," Jimmy said, without looking at me.

"We knew your parents," Annette said.

"Your Grandma . . . ," Jimmy said, trailed off.

"I imagine she's a lot," Annette said.

"A lot of what?" I asked, a little sharp.

"You know," Annette said.

"I don't know," I said.

"We knew Paul too," Jimmy said. "He's gained weight."

"Your mother beat me up for fun, once," Annette said.

"Your dad sold me weed, once," Jimmy said.

"Jimmy," Annette said. "Please."

Jimmy shushed her. The Bears fumbled on the goal line. Jimmy kicked the coffee table and a stack of coasters spilled on the carpet.

"Sometimes," I said, "I forget what they're like."

"That's not surprising," Jimmy said.

"I forget them also," Annette said.

"They're easy to forget," Jimmy said.

"I still love them," I said.

"Oh," Annette said. "Honey. Sweetie."

Annette put an arm around my shoulder, pulled me into her pointed ribs. I hated Annette.

"You should let them go," Jimmy said.

I hated Jimmy.

"They're my parents," I said.

"I left my parents," Annette said. "Years ago."

"They were horrible," Jimmy said.

"Just like your parents," Annette said.

"They were selfish," Jimmy said.

"Always about them," Annette said.

"No one else," Jimmy said.

"Horrible," Annette said.

"I still love them," I said.

Jimmy gave me a playful pinch behind my neck. I hated him more than before, more than anyone else. I felt sweat form on my nose and forehead. I wondered what would happen if I threw an elbow into Annette's porcelain ribs, if I pushed my head into Jimmy's lower jaw. I imagined a combat sequence that ended in me standing over their bruised and horrible bodies.

JANICE CAME IN with two dogs, a black German shepherd and something small resembling a teddy bear. The small one stood between the shepherd's front legs, looked proud, regal, adorable, ill at ease.

"Claude was just telling us about his family," Annette said to Janice.

Janice dropped the leashes. She was pale.

"Something bad outside," Janice said. "Cops everywhere."

"We didn't hear any sirens," Annette said.

"So?" Jimmy asked. "What's new?"

"Something bad is about to happen," Janice said.

Janice led us around the corner. The cops had blocked off the street. A crowd was gathering. Officer Baggs had an air horn to his face. He told everybody to respect da crime scene. Dis is a crime scene and we must not obstruct da police's efforts. I heard sobbing in the distance. Janice held my hand and grabbed my ass. An ambulance honked and the crowd parted. A small child lay motionless on the sidewalk. There wasn't any blood. I didn't remember hearing any gunshots.

"Murderers," someone yelled at Officer Baggs.

"What happened?" Annette asked the person closest to us, a middle-aged man in a Gale Sayers jersey.

"That boy stole something from the house," Gale Sayers pointed his chin toward a big brick house with a black fence. "The family was at church, or something. A neighbor called the cops. The cops came and the boy ran away, or something like that."

"Figures," Jimmy said.

"Jimmy," Annette said.

"I'm scared." Janice let go of my hand and wrapped her arms around me.

"So the cops come," Gale Sayers continued, "and they tackled the kid, because he isn't that fast. I think I've seen him before. Like running around the park, or something. If I'm thinking of the same kid, if I saw him before, I know he isn't that fast."

"That's the Warrens' boy," someone else said. "He wasn't stealing anything. He was just going in to feed the cats because the family is out of town. The Warrens are good people."

"So I have seen him before," Gale Sayers continued. "I knew I had seen him before. So long story short, the cops catch the kid and sit on him because the kid won't cooperate. They sit on him so the kid can't run away. But they end up suffocating him. They were choking him too, I think."

"Murderers!" Jimmy yelled at the cops. The crowd grew. Officer Baggs yelled for order. He said that we must keep da peace at all costs. Someone threw a football at Officer Baggs. He ducked and reached for his gun. Then four SUVs screeched to a stop behind us. The Redbelters jumped out.

"Pigs!" Annette yelled at the cops.

Big Columbus climbed onto the hood of an Escalade.

"Are we going to take this?" Big Columbus asked the crowd. Everyone faced him, even the cops and paramedics.

"Are we going to remain victims?" Big Columbus asked.

"No," someone yelled back.

"Are we going to let these criminals kill our babies, our little sisters and brothers?" Big Columbus stomped on the hood.

"If we don't do something about this today," Big Columbus said, "then we won't have a tomorrow. We have fallen prey to these evildoers, and they will not stop until they have taken everything we have."

"We need power," someone yelled back.

Janice put her face in my armpit and bit me.

"We must destroy them," Big Columbus said, "before they destroy us."

Riot

////////

BEFORE US: COPS and more cops lined up in combat gear. Everyone not in church was standing in the street, staring down every cop in South Shore. I recognized some cops, even in their helmets, behind their shields. I didn't know their names, just their faces. When I was seven, I'd seen a patrolman pistol whip a boy in handcuffs right on Sixty-Eighth and Bennett. The boy was breaking into cars. Now, I saw the same patrolman looking anxious and armored, poised to deal blows. He was standing in the vanguard. Was he always brutal? I tried to turn around with Janice. I wanted to run, but I couldn't seem to. I moved too slowly. Big engines pumped and howled, tires screeched like wounded large birds.

Behind us: Redbelters and more Redbelters pulled up in black trucks.

We, the civilians, were trapped in the middle, about twenty of us sucked into the standoff, squished.

"Look at these pathetic soldiers!" Big Columbus yelled. "They want war!"

The Redbelters formed a line at their cars' thick front bumpers, mirrored the cops. Big Columbus remained standing on his hood, organized his soldiers. Their numbers were similar. Their demeanors too—anger radiated off their heads. Just like the cops, they were ready. Except the Redbelters didn't have armor, helmets, shields, and automatic weapons. The Redbelters had handguns tucked, visible, in their waistbands. They carried blunt instruments.

"Move!" Big Columbus yelled.

The Redbelters took two steps.

"Stop!" Big Columbus yelled.

The Redbelters stopped.

I saw familiar faces in the Redbelters camp. Frank Wooten had a baseball bat at his side; Herc, a frying pan; Bobby, from the gas station, a broom; Little Brian, a hockey stick.

"DISPERSE," a bullhorn said.

The cops inched closer.

"Look at these puppets!" Big Columbus yelled to us civilians. "They want to invade our streets!"

We civilians responded. The Redbelter soldiers remained silent, tapped their weapons on the ground, on their chests, in their palms. They looked different from humans. All that anger and bloodlust turned them animatronic, like the cops.

"He's right!"

"This is our neighborhood!"

"Our streets!"

"They don't care about you!" Big Columbus yelled.

"He's right!"

"They want to kill us!"

"No!"

"Wait!"

"Everybody calm down!"

"No!"

"DISPERSE," a bullhorn said.

"Fuck the cops!"

"They killed that boy!"

"Talk!"

"Don't kill!"

"They want to kill us!"

"Brothers and sisters!" Big Columbus yelled. "Take back your sidewalk. Take back your pride. Make your own history! Eradicate the virus!"

"DISPERSE," a bullhorn said.

"They killed my cousin two years ago!"

"They killed my brother!"

"They killed Fred Hampton!"

"*You* disperse!"

Big Columbus jumped off the hood of his car. He stood with his soldiers. I held Janice tighter than she held me. Jimmy and Annette stood at attention, focused on Big Columbus. Everyone looked at Big Columbus. He had a general's air. The cops maintained their formation behind us. I felt my heart beating against Janice's back. I felt her heart in my arms. My eyes darted between the cops and the Redbelters. A few civilians walked behind the Redbelter phalanx. A few civilians tried to find security behind the cops. The cops held up their shields and wouldn't let them through. The refused joined Big Columbus, were welcomed like family by the Redbelters. I considered which side to seek out. I tried to consider what was at stake. The lines between right and wrong seemed blurred and indecipherable. What was everybody saying? How was this supposed to end?

"Let's go," Jimmy said.

"Damn right," Annette said.

Jimmy and Annette pulled Janice from my arms and dragged her toward the Redbelters.

"Claude!" Janice yelled.

More civilians tried to break police ranks.

"We're on your side!"

"Let us through!"

"Help us!"

"DISPERSE," a bullhorn said.

Soon, it was just me in no man's land.

Why wouldn't the cops accept us? I could see the officers' faces underneath their riot helmets. Couldn't they see our fear? Why didn't they let us through? Black cops too, standing there blank and emotionless. Why weren't they scared? Why wasn't everyone scared like me? I got angry at the cops' blankness.

And, then, I wanted them to fear me, to fear us, to understand our capabilities.

Instead, they pushed us away.

"DISPERSE," a bullhorn said.

"Claude!" Janice yelled again.

I lost sight of her.

Now, all these years later, all my inner chaos remains hard to decipher. Why didn't I join her and Jimmy and Annette? Why was I stranded? I couldn't move. Why? Did I feel trapped in history, between two violent wrongs? There was no available peace. Throughout high school, my history teachers wouldn't explain what happens when there's no available peace. When they kill one of yours and you want to defend yourself. Big Columbus just wanted to free us. And you can't ask for freedom. And we're free because of it. We didn't ask. A war was fought over freedom over a century ago. People said, when they wanted to sound smart in history class, those people in the front row, they said: "The Civil War wasn't fought over slavery, to free black America." They said, "The Civil War was political." And they said, "Black America still isn't free." And then other people have said Martin Luther King was a revolutionary—not some singing pacifist. They've said, "Nonviolent protest was political." They've said, "Nonviolent protest was meant to show the world how violent the white man was, how backward the South was. What about the North? What about Chicago? Martin Luther King said he saw worse racism, worse discrimination, more evil in the North, in Chicago." And they've said, "Martin Luther

King was a puppet." And these people who've said Martin Luther King was a puppet have also said, "Brother Malcolm got it right: any means necessary." And both those brothers got shot. And both those brothers wanted freedom. And the Civil Rights Act was political. And black America still isn't free. And black men are still dying. And black women are still dying. And there's anger, yes, there's anger. And that anger has to go away when you go to work or go to school or ride the bus or go to the grocery store or go to a movie downtown. And that anger has to go away—if it doesn't, how do you survive?

And there I was, that early afternoon, alone, feet stuck, unable to escape.

During the riot, everybody was angry as hell. And that anger was confusion. And confusion is dangerous when you're standing in the middle of the street and not sure if you should go with the gang that kills people or the cops that kill people. And there's only one option.

And that option is standing with your people.

We're free. We're free. We're free. We're free. History says we're free. We're free.

"DISPERSE," a bullhorn said.

And I went looking for Janice.

"Janice," I yelled.

"Claude," Janice yelled back.

"Annette," Janice yelled back.

"Jimmy," Janice yelled back.

"Are you all dead?" Janice asked.

I still couldn't see her. Big Columbus clapped his hands.

"Brothers and sisters!" Big Columbus yelled at his allies. "You see how they pushed you away. You see the hate in their souls. We must rid ourselves of these vermin, these vile scourges! Join me! Rise with me!"

The crowd responded with cheers.

"DISPERSE," a bullhorn said.

"Dismantle the oppressor!" Big Columbus yelled.

He pointed and then his allies ran toward the cops. I stayed on the sidewalk, still looking for Janice.

The tear gas came the moment the two sides collided. This was an old battle scene. Hand-to-hand and unforgiving. The Redbelters kept their guns tucked. The cops smashed their riot sticks indiscriminately against torsos and skulls. The tear gas plumed and drifted over the throng. Fighting continued through coughing and hacking. Everyone was clumped together and hurting. I saw a hockey stick break against a riot shield. I saw a skull break against a riot stick. I saw cops don gas masks and descend upon coughing and blind fathers and mothers and brothers and sisters and big cousins and uncles and nieces and aunts and nephews. I saw no peace.

"Janice!" I yelled.

No response.

"Janice!" I yelled again.

"Fight!" Big Columbus yelled. "Fight for your freedom!"

"DISPERSE," a bullhorn said.

"Janice!" I yelled again.

"DISPERSE."

I saw a blinded and coughing woman break a cop's leg with a shovel.

I saw a blinded and coughing man spin his arms like windmills against a riot shield.

I saw mounted horsemen on the horizon.

I saw helicopters above.

I saw madness and confusion.

I saw humanity collapse in on itself.

I was scared.

I was alone.

"Janice!" I yelled one last time.

I dispersed.

I ran home.

I ran past family homes, homes of friends, brothers, and sisters.

There were the Jacksons with their three toddlers. The Jackson parents were professors of medieval literature at Chicago State. Their oldest son died of cancer when he was thirteen.

SWAT trucks sped past.

There were the Mitchells, an old couple that organized block parties and neighborhood-wide garage sales because they wanted the community to remain intact.

The Howards and their four-story blue stucco. Their daughter was in my grade. She stuck gum underneath her desk every day. She had bad breath and said gum made her feel normal. Mrs. Jamaica would have given her detention if she found out.

The Smith and Williams families gathered around the picket fence that divided their houses. They hated each other because the Smiths' dog liked pissing on Mr. Williams's roses and shitting next to Mrs. Williams's garden gnomes.

No one noticed me. I could hear faint screaming over the sirens, gunshots, and helicopter blades.

I tripped and fell on the Billings' lawn. The Billings had moved back to Virginia after their twins graduated from private schools last May. Their grass was overgrown. Their bushes were dying. The For Sale sign had a giant spiderweb in between the posts. People didn't want to buy houses in South Shore. They wanted to buy apartments in Bucktown.

A large blast, like a bomb, went off. I turned and saw flames. The families ran back into the houses. I was alone on the street. I saw a burning man running toward me. He dropped. People smacked the burning pile with their coats and feet. I ran home with my eyes half-closed, tripping every couple of steps.

Grandma was standing on our porch in her Sunday dress and church hat. A wooden plank rested on her shoulder like a musket.

"Where's Janice?" I asked.

"She's inside with Paul," she said. "And, why the hell are you not inside?"

Janice sat on the living-room floor wrapped in a blanket.

Paul, in his suit and on his stomach in front of her, wiped the blood from her shins.

"You guys should've come to church," Paul said, with a nervous smile.

I fainted.

When I came to, Grandma was an inch away from my face.

"Those motherfuckers," she whispered. "Those motherfuckers."

Paul had Janice in his arms on the couch.

"Is it over?" I asked. A frozen pork chop was on my forehead. I looked down at my chest. The blood was still wet.

"It'll never be over," Grandma said. "The National Guard is coming."

Grandma stood, used her wooden plank like a crutch.

"Bush might send the air force," Paul said.

"Everybody's dead," Janice said. Her eyes slammed shut.

"Not everybody," Paul said. "But a lot."

A knock at the door.

"Don't think you're getting in here!" Grandma yelled.

"Is Janice there?" a voice asked.

"Who the fuck is asking?" Grandma yelled back.

"Annette!" Annette yelled.

Grandma opened the door.

Annette.

She was covered in dust. She looked like a ghost. Her face was hollow. She wasn't dead.

"Is Jimmy here?" Annette asked. "Where's Jimmy? Our house is empty and the windows are broken."

She noticed Janice and ran to the couch. She kneed Paul in the stomach by accident. He pretended he wasn't hurt. I sat up.

"I think Jimmy's dead," Annette said.

She held Janice's head against her chest, spoke into her hair.

"I'll go get some water," Paul said.

"Turn on the TV," Grandma said.

South Shore was on every channel. News cameras from the helicopters showed burning houses and burning lawns; people running scared, people standing their ground; cops advancing, cops retreating; firing guns, tear gas, leaking wounds, charging horses.

Each channel had a different headline.

BREAKING: POLICE KILL CRIMINAL. NEIGHBORS RIOT.

BREAKING: GANGMEMBERS KILL OLD WOMAN. POLICE OVERWHELMED.

BREAKING: DEATH OF UNARMED BLACK TEEN IGNITES VIOLENCE.

BREAKING: CHICAGO BURNS.

Paul carried five opened bottles of wine into the living room and handed us each one.

"This," Paul said, "is nothing compared to when MLK died."

"Paul," Grandma said. "They're kids."

"They're fourteen," he said. "The world is about to end. A little Riesling won't hurt."

I drank from my bottle. So did Grandma. So did Paul. Janice

and Annette held theirs with shaking hands and stared at the aerial footage.

"Remember the Democratic convention?" Paul said.

"Paul," Grandma said. "This is bad enough."

"I know," Paul said, "but this is nothing like sixty-eight."

"It's worse," I said.

"What do you know?" Paul asked me.

"This is our neighborhood," I said.

"What does that have to do with it?" Paul asked me.

"The cops are occupying our neighborhood," I said.

"You sound like that Big Columbus fool," Paul said.

"The cops wouldn't leave," I said. "The cops wanted a war. They wanted to kill more of us."

"How do you know?" Paul said.

"I saw it," I said.

The aerial footage followed four teenagers running down Sixty-Seventh Street toward the epicenter.

"Hooligans looking for action," a newscaster said over the footage.

They carried duffle bags and had their black hoodies up. I wondered if I knew them. I wondered if I should join them. As they ran, they took turns pulling out liquor bottles from their duffle bags. There were rags stuffed in the bottles. They took lighters to the rags and tossed the bombs at parked cars.

"Horrible, horrible," a newscaster said.

"You see?" Paul asked me.

"Is that Monica's son?" Grandma asked. "Those knuckle-heads are going to start World War Three, Four, and Five."

"At least they're doing something," I said.

"This?" Annette asked. "This is something?"

In history class, we talked about gunfire during World War I, constant and pounding, so constant and pounding you forget it's there, forget death is flying over your trench. Looking at the live footage, those teenagers exploding cars, I stopped paying attention to the gunfire outside. Where were they heading with that explosive cargo? Those teenagers, my age—what did they know that I didn't? There they were: heading into the maelstrom I fled. Brave and strong, they were unstoppable.

The teenagers approached a line of riot-geared cops.

"Don't do it," Grandma said to the TV.

We could see the cops, guns raised, yelling at the teenagers. We could see the teenagers standing side by side. We could see a paper bag flutter between them, fallen leaves swirling skyward. We could see our neighborhood aflame.

We couldn't hear what the cops were yelling. We couldn't hear their hearts beating. I couldn't hear anything over the blood rushing behind my ears.

The teenagers pulled their hoods down.

And it was Monica's son. And it was Travis. And Chin. And Mary Dobson.

"I know them!" I shouted.

And then Mary Dobson reached into her duffle bag.

And the cops fired into their teenage bodies.

And they wouldn't stop.

The screen cut back to the studio. A newscaster looked pale.

"We apologize," he said. "That was—what a—terrible—"

Janice dropped her bottle. Annette held Janice tighter.

"He's not there," Grandma said. "Don't worry. He's not there."

"Where is he?" Annette asked. "Where is he? Where is he? Where is he?"

"Our hearts go out to those in Chicago," the newscaster continued. "We'll be back with more from South Shore."

A commercial for enlarged-bladder medication came on. A fire truck passed by our house. I noticed the gunfire again, then, and forever. I thought of things I would die for. All of them were beside me.

Nothing changed when the sun went down. Paul tried to order pizza. We heard the guy laughing at him through the phone when Paul told him the address. Grandma decided to make bacon and eggs.

"We never got breakfast," Grandma said.

Annette and Janice didn't move from the couch. I was almost done with my Riesling and felt tired and sick. Paul was on his second bottle. He was smoking on the porch because Annette's head hurt. Bush was scheduled to address the nation at nine. Jimmy was still missing.

"We don't need to watch this anymore," Grandma said. "We know what's happening. Let's eat."

Grandma finished cooking the eggs, walked into the living room, turned off the TV, stuck the remote in her bra.

"Claude," she said. "Get Paul."

Paul leaned over the railing. A burning cigarette was next to his foot.

"Do you see that?" he asked. "I wouldn't mind that being the last thing I ever see."

The smoke in the distance looked like heavy mist. Helicopters shone spotlights down on the wreckage. We couldn't see any of the fighting. We could hear sirens and gunshots behind the peaceful houses and apartment buildings in front of us. Cop cars and trucks drove up our street. One of them stopped. The officer told us to get back inside. "At night," the cop said, "it's only going to get worse."

"Let me enjoy this," Paul said.

"If you're drunk," the officer said, "I can take you to jail. Go inside."

Then he drove off. I stood with Paul a second longer. Then I pulled his arm and told him breakfast was ready.

"Is it morning already?" he asked. "I thought I was only out here for twenty minutes."

Grandma had plates ready for us.

"I was just telling Annette that I thought you died in sixty-eight," Grandma said to Paul.

"I was hiding," he said. "Jimmy is probably hiding."

"You hear that?" Grandma asked.

"But I did almost die," Paul said. "Jimmy could be dead."

"Paul," Grandma said.

Janice poked her eggs with a fork.

Paul told us about sixty-eight.

First, Martin Luther King got shot. Grandma and Mom had just moved in with Paul. Mom was a baby. Paul was working on a photo series about urban decline.

"No one knew what was going on," Paul said. "If you didn't live in a city, you had no idea what us black folks were doing. I knew black country folks that saw black city folks as a mystery. I got a commission from some Podunk gallery in Texas. I took my camera to opened fire hydrants, got pictures of children playing, jumping rope, that kind of thing. I took my camera up to the Rucker. I took pictures of people going to the movies. Just normal stuff that everyone does. I was saying, with my work, I was saying, 'Look, urban decline isn't caused by the individual urbanite. It's the urban *institution*. The individual urbanite is just like everyone else when it comes down to living life.' Government is the problem. Capitalism is the problem. We were all Communists back then. So I was shooting these photos, trying to humanize and contextualize. And then they go ahead and kill Martin.

"I was taking photos that night. And it was just like today. I thought I'd go out there and join the struggle, join my brothers. Just like today: cars on fire, shop windows broken, running, screaming, crying, sadness, fear, disbelief, anger—all that rolled into one roving blaze. I hid underneath a car for three days.

"After Bobby Kennedy got killed, your grandma got a modeling job in Chicago. She wanted a friend and babysitter to move with her. You know, back then, it was just me and Catherine and your mother, all day, every day. We didn't have any other friends. We didn't want any. When Catherine moved, of course, I was going to move with her. We were platonic vagabonds.

"We moved to South Shore August 1, 1968. The Democratic convention came to Chicago three weeks later.

"I was babysitting your mother," Paul said. "And I thought I'd just pop up to Grant Park, you know, say what's up to some friends, yell a little, get back home in a couple hours. Two hours, tops. I left your mother with our neighbors, these Jewish folks down with the struggle. Old Communists. Fuck Nixon. Fuck Vietnam. That kind of thing. And I went up north. Mayor Daley unleashed those cops on us like Hades unleashing Cerberus. I got the fuck out of there."

"What's your point?" I asked.

"My point is: stay out of it," Paul said to me. "There's enough trouble waiting for you. Don't go looking for it."

"Jimmy's not dead," Grandma said to Annette.

We picked at our eggs. Paul stood up to get more wine from the basement. Grandma made him sit down. Annette went into the living room. Janice was frozen and unresponsive. I was drunk and dizzy.

"Look what you did," Grandma said to Paul. "You're torturing that poor woman."

"This isn't anything," Paul said. "This is *Romper Room*."

Annette told us all to come quick.

"Hurry," she said. "They're coming right for us."

Our street was on TV. Outside our window helicopter searchlights weaved. The TV shook. They cut to the news anchor.

"Again, we remind all South Shore residents to stay inside," he said.

Breaking glass and car alarms. They went to commercial. Lexus had a sleek new hybrid that got fifty miles per gallon on the highway.

"Claude," Grandma said. "Take Janice and Annette to the basement."

Grandma picked up her wooden plank, told Paul to grab a knife, and walked outside.

AFTER FIVE MINUTES Paul came running down the stairs empty handed.

"It's about to happen," he said.

"What about Grandma?" I asked.

"It's a nightmare up there," he said.

Annette pulled Janice into a closet. Paul tried to push me into a corner. I slipped under his arms and ran upstairs. Paul was right. It was a nightmare. The front door was open. Grandma stood on the porch with her wooden plank raised like a bat. I picked up the knife Paul had dropped on the carpet and joined her.

A teenager stood in front of our house with a glass bottle aimed at Grandma.

"Try it," Grandma said. "I'll split you down the middle."

He broke the bottle on the sidewalk and took off laughing. Grandma turned around.

"If you're going to help," she said, "don't stand back there."

She made room for me at her side. The riot moved like a herd. I saw someone get trampled. I saw someone pull shoes off a lifeless body. I saw cops cursing a handcuffed boy. I saw a cop drop his riot shield, take off his helmet, and run toward the lake. I saw despair unbound.

"If someone gets close enough," Grandma said, "don't hesitate to use that."

I DIDN'T HAVE to kill anybody. Grandma didn't kill anybody either. We didn't leave our house for two days. As promised, Bush sent in the National Guard. Janice slept in my room, Annette in Grandma's. Paul stayed in the basement. I slept under a large blanket in the living room with Grandma. The fighting erupted in random spurts. We slept in shifts. I thought Janice would look at me like I was a hero. But she wouldn't talk to me, or anyone.

When it was safe enough, on the third morning, I went with Grandma to Annette and Janice's house. Annette and Janice stayed back. They didn't want to know how much they'd lost. They didn't want to find Jimmy's body on the street. Paul stayed back.

On the walk we passed reporters sifting through the wreckage like archaeologists. SWAT members with assault rifles were at every corner.

Without any bombs dropping, the neighborhood was bombed out. Most street-facing windows were broken. A few cars were turned over, blackened with fire. Thin saplings had been torn from the earth; bushes were reduced to twig piles. Overhead, the trees, somehow, had lost their lowest-hanging leaves. Those same trees had deep scars in their old bark. We were now used to the sounds around us. We didn't flinch when, somewhere up the street, a man wailed and cursed God. We remained calm when a helicopter sped toward rapid gunfire.

"Can you believe people?" Grandma asked me.

"Huh?" I asked.

"All this destroyed nature," Grandma said.

She stepped over a trampled squirrel.

From the sidewalk, Annette and Janice's place was a ruin. Of course, the windows were broken. Bullet holes dotted the facade. Their front lawn, somehow, had been stripped and was half dirt.

"You ready?" Grandma asked me at the front door.

"Maybe," I said.

"Same," Grandma said, turned the key Annette had given her.

Even in daytime, the foyer was dark. Bird shit and awful smells covered the furniture and walls. Bullets had found their way inside and exploded picture frames and vases.

"Their rooms are upstairs," I said.

"Move," Grandma said.

We hurried to the second floor.

The destruction didn't extend up there. On the landing, however, we heard barking, then whimpering, then barking.

"There," I said, pointed to an opened door.

"Careful," Grandma said.

In the bedroom, on a king-size bed, the two dogs were curled into one mound. The little dog was tucked into the big dog's stomach. Family photos were on the dresser, nightstands, blown-up large and hung on the walls. The dogs growled when I tried to get close. The little one showed her teeth. They seemed unhurt, just thin and scared. Grandma joined me. They didn't growl at her.

"Poor babies," Grandma said. "Come here, poor babies. Come."

First, the little one unspooled from the big one, jumped down, and ran into Grandma's arms. Grandma scooped her up, and the big one jumped down too, rubbed its large black head against Grandma's calves.

"What now?" I asked.

"Find some garbage bags," Grandma said. "They need clothes."

The fridge was ajar and empty; cabinets were opened and cleaned out; flies formed a cloud over the rotten trash can; I found a dead rat on the stove, uncooked, bloated. Under the sink, I found garbage bags and sprinted upstairs.

Grandma was on the bed, on her back, with a dog on either side. She rubbed their heads and shushed their whimpers, calmed their growls when I entered.

"What now?" I asked.

"Find Janice's room," Grandma said. "Fill a bag."

Janice's room was up the hall, a KEEP OUT sign drilled into the door. Once, I had a dream about her room, in which we had sex on silk sheets underneath a lace canopy. In my dream, there was a hot tub near the bed, a sunflower patch growing downward from the ceiling.

Standing in her open doorway, in reality, I smelled musk, dried sweat. Her clothes were arranged in piles across the floor. There were posters of faraway cities, European and Asiatic. On a small desk, textbooks still wrapped in plastic were stacked up to my chin. From her window, I saw their backyard: a destroyed garden and caved-in garage. Her bed was unmade. I climbed in. Her sheets were hard and made me itch, the musk's source. I held my breath, closed my eyes, and rubbed my head into her pillow.

Grandma and the dogs woke me up.

"Whatever you're doing," Grandma said, "cut it out and get moving."

We filled the garbage bags with clothes and underwear and went back. The dogs, without leashes, stayed at Grandma's side.

At home, Annette and Janice tried to pet their dogs, but they stayed at Grandma's side.

The final body count was twenty-six. Some cops. Some Redbelters. Of course, Jimmy and people like Jimmy. Trapped people that were looking for a place to run and ended up in the crossfire. Jimmy was shot three times. Janice had to identify the body in our high school's gym. They had the bodies lined up across the basketball courts. Jimmy's was close to the free-throw line.

There was a mass memorial in Grant Park that no one in the neighborhood could go to. The buses weren't running. And it was after curfew.

IN THE FOLLOWING weeks, everyone talked about South Shore. Grandma kept the news playing. Reporters talked about brutal police and our militarized state. Senator Obama vowed to take legislation to Washington. He said he would help us rebuild and reconstruct. Jesse Jackson walked around with camera crews. Grandma said he used to live in South Shore; Grandma said he was worse than politicians. Bush even visited. He gave a speech at our high school and the teachers booed. Mayor Daley handed out turkeys on Thanksgiving.

Big Columbus disappeared, sent videos to CNN. In one of them, while he spoke against police states, his followers shot human-size cardboard targets in a flat and barren field. They were sweating through military fatigues. They looked unwell, sick and thin.

Officer Baggs got promoted to sergeant.

After a month, the news moved on. Haiti fell into another civil war. A tsunami poured over Japan. School started back up. The National Guard left. The Red Cross moved on. Families that still had homes threatened to move away but didn't. Jesse Jackson and Senator Obama disappeared again.

CHRISTMAS CAME WITHOUT presents.

By that point Janice had taken over my bed. I had a cot that my feet hung off of. Annette had a room in the attic that she hated because it was filled with spiders and dusty books. The dogs slept with Grandma.

I would try to kiss Janice at night. Or I'd reach my hand over to touch her thigh.

"Not now," she would say. "Try again tomorrow."

For New Year's, Paul bought everybody their own bottle of champagne. When the champagne was gone we sat on the living room floor and picked at a chocolate cake.

"Do you think Claude and Janice will get married?" Annette asked.

"Why not?" Paul said. "They could both do worse."

"Yeah," Annette said that Christmas. "If they got married Janice would never leave South Shore."

"Claude's going to make a difference in this world," Grandma said.

"Both of their parents are awful," Annette said.

"My daughter's not awful," Grandma said. "She's just ridiculous."

"Should we talk about our ruined lives?" Paul asked.

"Do you have any answers?" Grandma stared at Paul and he looked away.

"I'm just saying," Paul said to the carpet.

Vacuum

//////////////////////////

AFTER A YEAR, Annette couldn't take it anymore.

"I feel his ghost," she said. "I feel it all the time."

Some nights, I could hear her in the attic, pacing, crying, talking to the walls and spider webs. Some nights, she screamed in her sleep. We would take turns, run upstairs, shake her awake, sit at her side. When she screamed, the dogs barked. Those nights it felt like we were under attack again. All that noise and hurrying feet.

She had to leave South Shore.

She met a man with four daughters. This man got a job in California.

Grandma and Annette argued in the attic. Janice, Paul, and I listened through my ceiling.

"And Janice?" Grandma said. "What about Janice?"

"She's happy here," Annette said.

"No one's happy," Grandma said.

Someone dropped something heavy above our heads.

"I'm taking the dogs," Annette said.

"You're what?" Grandma asked.

"They're Jimmy's dogs," Annette said. "They're all I have left."

"What about Janice?" Grandma asked again.

"They're my dogs," Annette said.

Someone stomped, over and over, above our heads, in a circle, over and over.

The next morning, Annette leashed the whimpering dogs, put her packed bag at the front door. Janice packed her own bag, blocked Annette's exit. Soon, Annette's ride would pull up.

"Can't I come?" Janice said.

"You'll just remind me of him," Annette said to Janice.

Grandma pulled Janice away from the door, took her place, stood before Annette. Paul and I watched from the kitchen, poised to join. Grandma bent down to pat and shush the dogs, tell them she loved them.

"Leave," Grandma said, without looking up, to Annette. "Now."

Annette dragged the unwilling dogs outside.

On the curb, Annette waited for her new life. Snow swirled around her. A sleek new Lexus hybrid pulled up and took her to a different place. Who knows whether that place was better.

Janice moved into the attic.

The riot took the romance out of us. We all came out less full, drained. We all felt Jimmy's ghost.

When Big Columbus disappeared, he didn't take the drugs with him, or the guns, or his child soldiers, my classmates. He took the organization with him. The corner boys and girls lost direction. The cops moved in, stationed more undercovers at the bus stops, in the parks, in the apartment-building courtyards. Arrests were up. Still, arrests weren't the problem.

Gangs from other territories tried to claim South Shore. Both nations, Folk and People, wanted to supply South Shore with dope and guns. Even the Hispanic gangs from Logan Square, Pilsen, and Humboldt wanted some action—MS-13 and Latin King graffiti showed up in alleyways. In the resulting struggles, seventy people were killed in July; most of them were kids my age; too many of them were just in the wrong place at the wrong time heading in the wrong direction.

"What do you mean 'leave'?" Janice asked. She craned her head out my open bedroom window, looking for a gunshot's origin. I watched her from my bed.

"Leave," I said. "Like *go.*"

"But where?" Janice asked. "But how?"

"College, probably," I said.

Janice fell back in the window when another gun went off, and then another, and then three more.

"Think they're down by the beach," Janice said.

"I can't stay here anymore," I said.

"It's always been bad," Janice said. "When hasn't it been bad?"

"Who wants to live like this?" I asked.

"Like what?"

"Like, crazy, unpredictable, like anything can happen at any moment."

"You're just dramatic," Janice said. "You're just grappling with existence."

"Aren't you?"

"Grappling with existence is stupid," Janice said.

"The city's going to close Crispus Attucks next fall," I said.

"Why do you care?" Janice asked.

"What if we're next?" I asked.

"Nothing's changed," Janice said. "You could have gotten shot walking down the street last year, two years ago, thirty years ago. Nothing's changed."

"Maybe Big Columbus was right," I said.

Big Columbus looked at history and understood loud people could make a difference, radical decisions could change the world.

"Him?" Janice said. "You think Big Columbus was right?"

"I think so," I said, and swallowed hard. "He wasn't given a chance."

"A chance?" Janice asked.

"To prove his point," I said. "To help the community."

"He's a murderer," Janice said. "He sells drugs."

"He didn't have a choice," I said.

"Everyone has a choice," Janice said.

"We have a good family," I said.

"Big Columbus took my family," Janice said.

"We have each other," I said.

"Big Columbus ruined my life," Janice said.

"We have opportunities," I said. "Not everyone has opportunities."

"What opportunities?" Janice asked. "What are my opportunities?"

"You could leave," I said. "Most people can't leave."

"Leaving won't make me happy," Janice said. "Leaving won't make you happy."

"It might," I said.

"Want to know about happiness?" Janice asked.

"I want to try," I said.

"If I had the chance," Janice said. "I would go back in time and kill them."

"Who would you kill?" I asked.

"All of them," Janice said. "Every Redbelter. I would bring them down."

"You couldn't," I said.

"Don't you understand?" Janice asked. "You're wrong about everything."

Janice stuck her head into the summer breeze. She watched the ambulances and cop cars holler past. I felt two massive forces pulling me in separate directions. I had to leave Chicago. I watched the blue and red lights flash against Janice's face. If she could time travel, I would go with her, do anything for her, except stay.

Chester Dexter and Renaissance

///

Sophomore year, after the bloody summer, after reading a flyer in the cafeteria, I joined the school newspaper,
Pantherbeat. The flyer promoted journalism as a great way to
see the world outside South Shore, expand your horizons.

After I told Grandma, she went up to her room and came
back with a book.

"Here." She threw a copy of Mike Royko's *Boss* at my chest.
It dropped on my spaghetti.

"That's going to be you," Grandma said. "A journalist. A
man of the people."

Paul applauded the prediction. Janice groaned at the sink and
ran the garbage disposal until there was nothing left to shred.

"I could work at a foreign bureau," I said. "In Rome or
Istanbul."

"Don't you see the state of your own people?" Grandma asked. "What do you care about Italians? What do you care about anyone else? We need you here."

"Everyone has problems," I said.

"Look after your own people," Grandma said.

"He wants to abandon us," Janice said.

"Write a story about me," Paul said. "Write a book about me and win a Pulitzer Prize."

My first assignment was to cover the freshman bake sale. They wanted to raise money for sweatshirts and sweatpants for their entire class. They didn't come close.

My second assignment was to write a feature about a retiring security guard. He was a Vietnam veteran. He told me about crawling after enemies through underground tunnels in total darkness. He told me how killing felt, all that power and sadness in his hands. At night, he said, in his bedroom, he could hear the jungle around him. "Still," he said, "all these years later, I can't forget." He wished his brain could be erased. My editor cut all the interesting stuff, said it was too adult.

My third assignment was about the softball team's horrible season.

The computer lab got a new projector—that was my fourth assignment.

I got fat from sitting at a desk all day.

JANICE GREW CURVED and full-lipped. She grew strong and indomitable. Sophomore and junior year she was a cheerleader. She went to parties all over the city. I was her lame brother; the athletes and rappers wanted me to put in a good word. I said I would and never did. Janice didn't need me anymore. Once, she brought me back a Styrofoam plate signed by Chief Keef.

She quit cheerleading before senior year. She started dating Chester Dexter, which was cooler than dancing on the sidelines. Chester Dexter scored more touchdowns than anybody else in Chicago. He even put up four hundred yards against Mount Carmel. Nobody put up four hundred yards against Mount Carmel. Chester Dexter showed Janice parts of Chicago I had only seen on TV. He could go to parties anywhere. Whenever he walked into a room people stared at his bulging neck and thighs like, Jesus, that boy is a horse.

I tried out for the basketball team and couldn't make it even though we were the worst team on the South Side.

Paul refused to meet Chester Dexter.

"If he ever hits you," he told Janice, "tell me and I'll find someone to break his knees."

Paul wanted Janice to date a basketball player. He thought football players were murderers and cheats.

One Saturday over winter break, Grandma wanted me out of the house.

"You're depressing me," Grandma said. "You need to party."

"I have to finish my applications," I said.

"You need to dance," Grandma said.

"These deadlines are coming up," I said.

"Let him stay," Paul said to Grandma. "He's my teammate."

Janice walked downstairs, beautiful, dressed up.

"Where you going?" Grandma asked.

"Out," Janice said, adjusted her earrings in the front window.

"With that boyfriend?" Paul asked.

"He's not my boyfriend," Janice said.

"Take Claude," Grandma said.

"I don't want to go," I said, even though I did. I wanted to see what her new life was like, if there was still room for me.

"He doesn't want to go," Janice said.

"He's just shy," Grandma said. "He's just stuck in his head."

"I don't want to go," I said.

"Why do you have to fill out applications?" Paul asked. "Didn't you already apply to DePaul?"

"Yeah?" Grandma asked me. "Don't waste your time."

"Fine," I said. "I'll go."

"Fine," Janice said. "He's almost here. Just try to act like someone cooler than yourself."

CHESTER DEXTER PULLED up in a charcoal Jeep. He made his friend sit in the back with me so Janice could sit up front and rub his knee with her hand. She had started putting sparkles in her nail polish. Football season was over.

"I'm all about scones now," Chester Dexter said as we pulled onto Lake Shore Drive.

His friend introduced himself as Renaissance. He looked thirty. But so did Chester Dexter.

"What's a scone?" Renaissance asked.

"It's like a muffin top," Chester Dexter said. "Except with more stuff happening."

"I could fuck with that," Renaissance said.

Renaissance gutted a tiny cigar with his fingernail, rolled down his window, and let cold wind pull the tobacco out. He filled it with weed, twisted it together in one motion, licked and sealed it, and tucked it into his sock.

"For sunrise." He smiled at me. His teeth were smaller than I expected.

"So, Claude," Chester Dexter asked through the rearview mirror, "what are you all about?"

"He doesn't know." Janice moved her hand to her hair.

"I like croissants," I said.

"Fancy boy," Renaissance said.

Chester Dexter turned up the radio. Janice moved her body in a way I hadn't seen before. She moved like another person, a person who was supposed to be sexy for football players.

We passed skyscrapers. Janice touched Chester Dexter's thigh, then chest, bicep, head. We pulled in front of an apartment building. On the curb I looked up and couldn't see the top. Chester Dexter left his car in a tow zone.

"The twins better have ginger ale," Renaissance said.

"I'm not buying shit," Chester Dexter said. Janice wrapped her arms around his waist. He walked into the lobby like he didn't notice her. I followed Renaissance. The doorman bowed to Chester Dexter. Chester Dexter flipped him his keys.

"Move it if the cops come," he said. "Don't touch it if they don't."

"Notre Dame needs more people like you," the doorman said. I turned around, and he was smiling at Chester Dexter's back.

Renaissance whistled Dixie as the elevator climbed. The twins lived on the top floor.

We stepped into a hallway filled with portraits of old white people in fancy clothes. They shined and their eyes followed you.

"We have arrived!" Chester Dexter took off. College scouts compared his speed to lightning. They were right. Renaissance put his arm around me. Janice followed Chester Dexter.

"This fancy enough for you?" Renaissance asked me. The portraits quivered as music shook the walls.

"What about the neighbors?" I asked.

"They're perpetually pissed," Renaissance said. We followed the music.

Renaissance knew where we were going. He dragged me along.

"What about their parents?" I asked.

"They have a house in Michigan," Renaissance said. "They're always there."

The twins' dining room table was set with ornate kitchenware. A large vase with wilted roses stood in the middle. We pushed open a swinging door and stood in the kitchen. The music was louder. Dishes were piled higher than the sink. The bass shook and an unsteady plate fell to the floor. It shattered. I slowed down and bent to clean it up. Renaissance kept pushing.

"Don't worry," he said. "That's not our duty. We're guests."

After the kitchen we arrived at a smaller library.

"This is the study," Renaissance said. "Hard drugs are studied here."

A large wooden door was on the other side of the study. I slowed down. Renaissance kept pushing.

"Are you ready?" he asked, and didn't give me time to answer. He opened the door and we walked into a mixture of cigarette, weed, and smoke-machine smoke.

About twenty teenagers were standing in a circle. All the lights were off except for a strobe. A disco ball hung from a chandelier. The chandelier, like everything else in the house, was antique. Underneath the disco-ball chandelier two boys were bareknuckle boxing. Music pumped from tall speakers in the room's four corners. I couldn't see Janice and Chester Dexter. Renaissance remained by my side. He yelled something at me I couldn't hear over the cheering and music. The smoke had reduced his face to a vague outline. But he was smiling, his teeth gleaming. The two fighting boys were outlines also. One knocked the other in the stomach and finished him off with an uppercut. I suspect the one that got knocked out hit the floor hard, but I couldn't hear it. A voice interrupted the music.

"Intermission," the voice said. The lights came on. The circle collapsed. When the music started again it was softer.

"Let's get some drinks," Renaissance said. He pushed through the crowd. I followed in his wake. There was a foldout table covered in wine bottles and liquor, a long cooler filled with ice and beer underneath the foldout table. Renaissance snaked to the front of the line and no one stopped him.

"Wine for the fancy boy?" he asked.

"Where's Janice?" I asked.

"No ginger ale." He put down a bottle of whiskey and picked up a beer.

"Where's Chester Dexter?" I asked.

"Dex's probably giving her the business." He handed me a plastic cup filled to the brim. Renaissance noticed something over my shoulder and looked scared.

"Let's move," he said. "The twins are coming."

We didn't get far before a hand grabbed my shoulder and turned me around. Renaissance disappeared into the smoke. Before me were two tall blonds. One of them was in a tight white dress with red wine stains down her chest. The other was in black. If she had similar stains, the black concealed them. I assumed she was stained also.

"You with him?" White Dress asked.

"I'm with Janice," I said.

"That's nobody," Black Dress said.

"She's like my sister," I said.

"If you're with him," White Dress said, "both of you have to leave."

"We hate him," Black Dress said. Black Dress's blond hair had pink streaks.

"He steals from us," White Dress said.

"If he steals from us," Black Dress said, "you steal from us."

"If you steal from us," White Dress said, "you fucking pay."

"Do you know Chester Dexter?" I asked. I was sweating and spilling my wine.

"Everybody knows Chester Dexter," White Dress said.

"Chester Dexter is famous," Black Dress said. "What are you?"

"I'm Claude." I extended my hand for a handshake. They backed away.

"Well, Claude," White Dress said.

"You're an intruder, Claude," Black Dress said.

"We have a crasher!" White Dress yelled, and the music stopped.

Everyone turned toward me. I looked for Chester Dexter or Janice. I hated Renaissance.

"You know what we do to intruders," White Dress said.

"Intruders must fight or leave," Black Dress said.

"I'll just leave," I said. I tried to walk past them.

"Did you not hear us?" White Dress asked.

"Let me find Janice," I said, "and we'll go."

"Intermission's over!" Black Dress yelled.

"Hold him," White Dress said to the guys standing around me. They obeyed.

The circle formed again. The guys carried me to the circle's edge. There was blood on the ground. Someone hit the lights and turned the music up. The voice came back.

"A slight change in our program," the voice said. "Up next: Intruder vs. Truck."

Through the strobe I couldn't see exactly what I was facing. It looked like a human man with gorilla arms and elephant shoulders. I caught flashes of his grimace. I thought he had a scar down the middle of his face. The twins put their heads on my shoulders.

"This is what happens when you steal from us," White Dress said.

"I didn't steal anything," I said.

"Truck is going to turn you into piss," Black Dress said.

"Are you going to kill me?" I asked.

They shoved me forward. A bell sounded and Truck lunged at me.

I waited for him to get close and slipped away. The crowd didn't like that. They booed me. They wanted blood. I kept looking for Chester Dexter and Janice. I heard Renaissance's voice.

Paul had tried to teach me how to fight in our basement. He taught me to kick shins and punch balls. Paul's techniques involved hiding kitchen utensils in his socks. He once pulled an orange peeler on me and demonstrated how to cut a throat.

"Kill him, Truck," Renaissance said. "Bury him, Truck."

I ducked around Truck and kicked his shins. That made him growl. I tried to punch his balls; I clipped his thigh, which felt like concrete wrapped in denim.

If all else failed, Paul told me to scream. Run and scream. Truck kept coming after me. I started screaming. So I was running around, kicking his shins, trying to punch his balls, and screaming as loud as I could. I might've looked like I was winning.

My legs were getting tired when Chester Dexter stepped into the circle.

"Enough!" he said. "Someone turn on the fucking lights."

Someone turned on the lights. Chester Dexter was between me and Truck.

Truck's scar zigzagged from his left temple to his right cheek. His eyes weren't demonlike, red, or pulsing. His eyes were emerald green. He was more sad than crazed. His neck was thicker than I thought. He breathed heavily.

"Who here is messing with my man?" Chester Dexter asked. "Who here is messing with me?"

Janice walked into the circle also. She adjusted her clothes and tried to tame her hair. The crowd went silent. The twins walked in front of Truck.

"He's an intruder," White Dress said.

"He steals," Black Dress said.

"Claude doesn't have stealing in him," Janice said.

"Just look at him," Chester Dexter said.

Everyone looked at me again. They seemed to agree. The circle dissolved; the party resumed. Some people wanted to shake my hand, acknowledge my balls.

"If that were me in there," a man with gauges in his ears and nose said, "I would've curled up into a ball and started crying."

Another person offered me a swig from their Hennessy bottle.

"Tonight is not your night," White Dress said to Chester Dexter and me.

"Come back when you drop the loser," Black Dress said to Chester Dexter.

Chester Dexter nodded in agreement.

"Renaissance!" Chester Dexter yelled. "We're moving out."

"Kofi's having a party," Janice said.

"Renaissance!" Chester Dexter yelled again. "Kofi's! Let's pop!"

Janice and Chester Dexter headed back toward the elevator. Renaissance caught up and slunk in behind them.

We rode the elevator in silence.

In the lobby, the doorman tossed Chester Dexter his keys.

"You bringing glory back to Notre Dame?" he asked Chester Dexter.

"Notre Dame can't afford me," Chester Dexter said.

"Brother," the doorman said, "no matter where you go, make sure you come back."

Chester Dexter dapped up the doorman. It was snowing outside. Janice curled underneath Chester Dexter's armpit.

"Does that ever get old?" Janice asked Chester Dexter.

"What?" Chester Dexter asked.

"All these people loving you," Janice said.

"They don't love me," Chester Dexter said. "They just want to know me."

In the backseat, Renaissance unpacked a porcelain ballerina statue from his jacket.

"Isn't it beautiful?" Renaissance asked.

"Try not to ruin our night," Janice said to me.

"I wasn't trying," I said.

"Don't worry about it," Chester Dexter said to me.

"Thanks for saving me," I said.

Janice rubbed Chester Dexter's face.

"Hero looks good on you," she said.

. . .

WE PARKED AND Chester Dexter got out. We followed. I understood why people loved Chester Dexter. It felt like right next to him was the safest place to be.

Kofi was Ghanaian. His parents were in the import business. He was standing in the doorway when we walked up.

"Chester Fucking Dexter," Kofi said. "Have everything you want. Everyone's in the basement."

He looked at me cross-eyed.

"Who's your man?" Kofi asked Chester Dexter.

"Dude knows numbers," Chester Dexter said. "He's gonna handle my money someday."

Kofi dapped me up, smiled, and showed yellow teeth.

"Anything you need," Kofi said to me.

Chester Dexter and Janice headed upstairs.

"Meet you in the basement," Chester Dexter said to Renaissance.

"Try not to start a war," Janice said to me.

Renaissance grabbed my arm.

"Come on," he said. He dragged me into the kitchen.

"What are you doing?" I asked.

He looked through the fridge. He sniffed fruit, opened Tupperware, tasted the milk.

"Come on," I said.

"Janice loves you," Renaissance said, with his head stuffed into a head of lettuce.

"What?" I asked.

"Janice," Renaissance said. "She talks about you all the time."

"She does?" I asked.

"You're her best friend," Renaissance said.

Renaissance finished with the fridge. He started looking through the cabinets.

"Why are you telling me this?" I asked.

"Dexter is cool," Renaissance said, "but he's not ready for the world."

"He seems ready," I said.

"You're ready," Renaissance said. "I can smell it on you."

"What is that supposed to mean?" I asked.

"You know," Renaissance said. "You got the musk."

Renaissance emerged from a cabinet with two bottles of Coke.

"Can't hide from me," Renaissance said to his discovery.

I accepted Renaissance as my guide; I followed him into the basement.

"There it is," Renaissance said. "There's what we want."

He pointed to a keg surrounded by liquor bottles.

He used me as a wedge through the crowd. I spilled someone's drink. Renaissance apologized on my behalf.

"He doesn't know any better," he said. "Fancy boy doesn't have any manners."

There was a line for the booze. Renaissance pushed us to the front.

"Give me that." He took the Coke out of my hands. "Let's forget who we are."

He picked up a bottle of vodka, took a swig from it, took a swig from the Coke, and passed the two bottles to me.

"Do it," he said.

I did as he said. I passed the bottles back to him. He repeated. I repeated. He repeated. I repeated. A guy with a Mohawk asked Renaissance if he could get some.

"This guy's sick with something incurable." Renaissance nodded toward me.

"But it's my bottle," Mohawk said.

"Do you want to die?" Renaissance asked.

Mohawk left us alone.

"You're alright," Renaissance said to me.

"I think you're a bad person," I said.

"That's true," he said. "But I could be worse."

"I'm going to throw up," I said.

"Figures," Renaissance said.

"Where's the bathroom?" I asked.

"I have to piss in the one down here," he said. "Go to the second floor. Don't get us kicked out again."

I put a hand over my mouth and took off.

Chester Dexter bumped into me when I was running up to the second floor. He shook his head.

"You're a pest," he said, and kept walking.

Janice was in the bathroom when I barged in.

"Jesus, Claude," she said. "Knock."

"I have to throw up," I said. "What were you doing?"

I barely made it to the toilet. Janice sat on the sink and laughed.

"Do you love me, Claude?" she asked. I couldn't answer.

"You want me all to yourself?" she asked. "Don't you?"

When I finished I looked up at her and saw that she was crying. I hadn't seen her cry since Jimmy died. She used to ask me questions like that all the time when she first became my sister. She'd walk into my room late at night and crawl into bed with me. Then I'd try to kiss her and she'd leave.

"When you look at me do you see something you want forever?" she asked.

I wanted to fall asleep on the bathroom floor. She flushed the toilet for me. She rubbed my back.

"You're a loser, Claude," she said. "You offer nothing."

"I know you love me," I said.

"What are you talking about?" she asked.

"Renaissance told me," I said.

"That guy huffs spray paint," she said.

"That's what I thought," I said.

She smiled and wiped her eyes on a hand towel. Then she wiped my mouth. She looked like she wasn't finished talking yet. Renaissance busted in.

"Get it together," he said. "Let's boogie. Dex is in the chariot."

The cops were downstairs yelling. Renaissance snatched a throw blanket off the couch on our way out.

In the car, Chester Dexter told us he was hungry.

"Maxwell Street?" Renaissance asked.

"Maxwell Street," Chester Dexter said.

MAXWELL STREET WAS right off the expressway and sold Polish sausages and pork chops and hamburgers twenty-four hours a day, seven days a week. I'd never been there that late on a Saturday. It looked like another party, which made me want to throw up again.

"Janice," Chester Dexter said when we pulled up. "Get us three Polishes and three burgers. And whatever you want."

"This is on me." Renaissance handed her two twenties. Janice slammed the door.

"Claude," Chester Dexter said through the rearview mirror, "Janice told me you fucked her."

"Chill," Renaissance said to Chester Dexter.

"I'm chill," Chester Dexter said. "I just want him to know that I know."

"It was only once," I said.

Chester Dexter didn't say anything. He watched Janice order.

"I think she's going to break up with me," Chester Dexter said.

Renaissance poked me in the ribs. Renaissance pulled the blunt from earlier out of his sock.

"Why you say that?" Renaissance asked.

"Just got the feeling," Chester Dexter said.

"That's just Janice," I said.

"Does she talk about me?" Chester Dexter said.

"Just about how cool you are," I said.

Renaissance passed me the blunt. Janice made her way back to the car. She handled her armful of greasy paper bags with grace and ease.

"I don't know," Chester Dexter said. "There's something about her I can't figure out."

"I know," I said.

"She loves you," Chester Dexter said to me.

"I know," I said.

We ate in near silence. Every now and then Janice would say something about how beautiful Chicago was at night. How she couldn't believe we got to live in a place this beautiful.

"Will you miss it?" she asked Chester Dexter. "Will you miss it when you're famous?"

"No," Chester Dexter said. "No. I won't. I'll miss you."

"Yeah," Janice said. "Right."

We finished eating. Chester Dexter drove us home. Renaissance was asleep and grinning when I got out of the car.

Paul and Grandma were both asleep in the living room. Paul was sitting up, snoring. Grandma had her head in his lap, snoring. We tiptoed up the stairs together.

"Do you think we'll be like that?" Janice asked outside my room. "Do you think we'll be together forever?"

"I don't know," I said.

"I hope not." She walked upstairs to her attic.

Ohio

////////////

A MONTH LATER, in March, I heard Janice break Chester Dexter's heart. They were underneath my window, on the front porch, smoking clove cigarettes.

"Can't you come with me?" Chester Dexter asked.

"To Ohio?" Janice asked.

"Yeah, everywhere."

"What am I going to do in Ohio with you?"

"You can be my girl."

"That's not something to do. That's not a reason."

"You can be rich," Chester Dexter said.

"That's something I can do on my own," Janice said.

"You can do anything you want," Chester Dexter said.

"I can do anything I want in Chicago," Janice said. "I can do anything I want anywhere I want."

"Then let's go to Ohio."

"You should go home."

"You're making a mistake," Chester Dexter said.

"No, I'm not," Janice said.

I heard Chester Dexter peel away in his charcoal gray Jeep. I heard Janice light another clove cigarette. I put on my slippers and rehearsed consoling lines. I heard the front door open.

"What's going on?" Grandma said.

"He wants to take me to Ohio," Janice said.

"That's too bad," Grandma said.

"We don't have anything to talk about," Janice said. "He just wants to look at me."

"That's all they ever want to do," Grandma said.

"If I went with him," Janice said, "I'd never have to work."

"Give me one of those," Grandma said. I heard Grandma light a clove cigarette. I heard Grandma cough.

"Am I stupid?" Janice asked. "Am I making a stupid mistake?"

"You know how many times I could've moved to Ohio?" Grandma asked. "You know how many men have asked me to move to LA, France, New York, Miami? Hell, one fool even tried to get me to follow him to Nebraska."

"Why didn't you go?" Janice asked.

"Because my life isn't about following men around," Grandma said. "And you know what happened when those fools moved away without me? You think they called, or wrote, or came back to visit?"

"They didn't," Janice said.

"Of course they didn't," Grandma said. "'Cause they were full of shit and scared of being alone in a new place. That's all. They're just scared and want us to help them."

"I'm scared too," Janice said.

"Damn right," Grandma said. "It's scary out in the world. You think I wasn't scared when I had a baby daughter and no family and no man and no money?"

"Then you met Paul," Janice said. "You found someone to help you."

"Paul," Grandma said. "Paul couldn't help himself to a free buffet. And I love Paul. When he dies, I'm going to grieve until I'm buried next to him."

"Claude is my best friend," Janice said.

"I know," Grandma said.

"I love him," Janice said.

"I know," Grandma said.

"He cares about me."

"I know," Grandma said.

"He understands me."

"I know," Grandma said.

"Ohio sounds awful," Janice said.

"I crashed a man's Corvette outside Cleveland," Grandma said.

I heard gunshots in the distance.

"Come on," Grandma said.

I closed my eyes and thought of the places I'd go with Janice, everywhere I'd follow her. I heard sirens get closer, closer, closer, closer, and speed by.

His sophomore year at Ohio State, Chester Dexter broke his leg in five places. I heard about it on TV. He moved back to Chicago and started selling used cars on Pulaski Road.

I haven't heard anything about Renaissance.

Denial and Acceptance

A WEEK AFTER Janice dumped Chester Dexter, my acceptance letter from Missouri came in a large envelope. I opened it at dinner.

"Without asking us?" Grandma asked.

"Why the hell would you apply to a place like that?" Paul asked.

"Without asking us?" Janice asked.

"I'm going," I said.

"No, you're not," Grandma said.

"Why would you do some stupid shit like that?" Paul asked.

"You're not going," Janice said.

"I can't stay in Chicago," I said.

"Yes, you can," Grandma said.

"All they got in Missouri is barbecue and guns and backward politics," Paul said.

"You can stay here," Janice said.

"It's the best journalism school in the country," I said.

"Northwestern," Grandma said. "Go to Northwestern."

"I didn't get in," I said.

"Apply next year," Janice said. "Take a year off."

"College is overrated," Paul said. "I can teach you anything you need to know."

"They have alumni networks all over the world," I said. "They have a study abroad program in Germany."

"Germany!" Grandma yelled.

"Expat!" Paul yelled.

"Why do you want to get so far away?" Janice asked.

"I can't stay here anymore," I said. "Don't you feel it?"

"Feel what?" Paul asked.

"Your insanity?" Grandma asked.

"Feel what?" Janice asked.

"Chicago doesn't want us!" I yelled. I stood and started for the doorway. I stopped and turned around before I walked out of the kitchen.

"They're closing schools," I said. "They're closing businesses. Obama isn't going to do anything. He can't do anything. No one can do anything. Tell me: is South Shore any better off now than it was ten years ago? Twenty years ago. Nothing is ever going to change. There's no way to change it. And the rest of the world isn't like this. We think the world is just like Chicago and it isn't. Civilization has moved on. The rest of the world isn't still corrupt, broken, wild, and dangerous. I could get shot any day for doing nothing. Just like that. Killed. *Bang*—walking down the street. The rest of the world isn't like this. We're trapped in this toxic bubble and we can't breathe and we think that's okay. What's wrong with us?"

I sat on the floor.

"Are you done?" Grandma said.

"Yes," I said.

"You're wrong," Grandma said.

"What?" I asked.

"The entire universe is ruined," Grandma said. "And no one wants us anywhere."

"I'm going," I said.

"If you leave," Grandma said, "you'll come right back."

"I won't," I said.

Grandma joined me in the doorway. She pulled me up.

"You will," Grandma said. "The world is no place for a self-hating black boy."

"Why won't you let me leave?" I asked.

"I'll let you leave," Grandma said. "And I'll let you come right back when everything goes wrong."

PAUL SHUFFLED INTO my room after dinner.

"I'm not staying," I said.

"Listen," Paul said. "We'll support you no matter how crazy your crazy-ass ideas are. We love you. We'll support you. I'm going to miss you. That's all. We're all going to miss you. Now, let us miss you."

Leaving and Asking

JANICE, GRANDMA, AND I were about to sit down for dinner when Paul came home with a fresh bruise on his face.

"Who kicked your ass?" Grandma asked.

"Love is a beast," Paul said to Janice and me. He ignored Grandma.

"What happened?" Janice asked.

"Who kicked your ass?" I asked.

"No swearing in the kitchen," Grandma said.

"He'll pay," Paul said, as he rummaged through the fridge.

"Who'll pay?" Janice asked.

Paul found a half-eaten grape bundle, some hummus, baby carrots, and blue Gatorade.

"Don't you want pork chops?" Grandma asked Paul.

"I gotta stay slim," Paul said. "I gotta stay fierce."

Paul moved upstairs, careful not to drop his haul. Out of sight, he dropped something, swore, dropped something else, cursed louder, dropped something else, slammed his door.

When dinner was fixed and on plates, Grandma sent me upstairs to make sure Paul was still alive.

"Grandma asks if you want broccoli," I said from his doorway. He was hunched over his desk with his back to me.

"A heavy hand is going to fall," he said.

"Can Janice have your broccoli," I asked, "if you don't want any?

"How's the list coming?" I asked.

"Almost done," he said. "Justice is about to bite someone. Right on the ass."

"Grandma wants to know if she should put an ice pack in the freezer," I said. "For your face."

"Yes," he said. "Please."

"Dinner's ready," I said.

"Tell Janice to stay off my broccoli," he said. "I'm in no mood."

He lifted his head up, didn't turn around.

"Can I do this?" he asked the wall.

"Grandma doesn't think so," I said. "Janice doesn't care."

"What do you think?" he asked.

"I think you can." I lied.

"Don't lie to me," he said. "I'm done."

"Can I see?" I asked.

He waved me over. The list wasn't really a list. It was one name, Charles Doyle, written ten times.

"Should I drive you to the hospital?" I asked.

"Charles Doyle is going to need a hospital," he said.

"Grandma thinks you should eat," I said.

"Where's my staff?" he asked. "I have to practice."

He'd bought the staff at a garage sale in Cicero. The woman said it was African and ancient. Paul paid sixty dollars. He threatened me with it whenever I called him insane. He pulled it out from under his bed.

"Leave," he said. "I must work."

"Should I put your food in the oven?" I asked.

"Yes," he said. "Warm my plate. Please. Thank you."

I heard him stomping his feet and yelling as I walked back down the stairs. That was a week before graduation. Grandma thought Paul was acting out because I was leaving for Missouri after summer.

After dinner I sat with her and Janice on the porch. Paul stomped around upstairs. His outline appeared and disappeared in the window.

"Who do you know in Missouri?" she asked.

"No one yet," I said. "I'm not there yet."

"What if all the people suck?" Janice asked.

"It's a big place," I said.

"Not that big," she said. "Not big like California, or Texas."

"Nothing is that big," I said.

"Are you going to stay there?" Janice said. "Will you stay forever?"

"Maybe," I said. "I don't know."

"You're soft," she said. "You deserve Missouri."

"You've never been there," I said.

"You're soft. You're going there. It's soft," she said. "It's cold. I'm going inside."

It wasn't cold. I followed her in.

Paul practiced with his staff all night. Something shattered when I was about to fall asleep. It sounded like the breaking of a lamp.

OVER BREAKFAST, JANICE told Grandma about her plans for after graduation. Paul was upstairs training.

"What do you mean you're not going to college?" Grandma asked.

"I want to work," Janice said.

"Doing what?" I asked.

"The service industry," Janice said.

"You want to serve people food?" Grandma asked. "What the hell is wrong with you two?"

"I want to be in control of my life," Janice said.

"That doesn't make any sense," Grandma said.

"It's more than just waiting tables," Janice said.

"You want to serve people alcohol?" Grandma asked.

"Some of those places downtown," Janice said, "the people that work there make six figures a year."

"Six figures?" Grandma asked. "When did you start talking like that?"

"Really?" I asked. "They make that much money?"

"Yeah," Janice said. "I met this guy at a party—"

"Claude," Grandma said. "Fuck out of here now."

PAUL WAS IN his room. He was sitting on his bed, out of breath.

"Did you do it?" I asked.

"Not yet," he said. "Can't leave anything to chance."

He threw himself onto the carpet and started doing push-ups. He got to four and a half and collapsed.

"What did you do to him?" I asked.

"Me?" he asked. He stood up.

"Yeah," I said.

"Me?" he asked again. He took a step toward me.

"You must've done something," I said.

"Me?" he asked again. "Me do something?"

"Yeah," I said. Our faces were almost touching.

"He took something from me," he said.

"What?" I asked.

"A man," he said. "He took a man from me."

"You don't have a man," I said.

"Correct," he said. "Not anymore."

"Janice and Grandma might kill each other," I said.

"Your mom was the same way," he said.

"How?" I asked.

"She wanted to kill Grandma," he said. "Grandma is unkillable."

He fell back down on the carpet and tried to do five more push-ups. He only made it to two. He rose to his knees.

"You know you're not going to see her?" he asked.

"Mom?" I asked.

"Or dad," he said.

"I don't even know where they are," I said.

"Just checking," he said. "They don't want to see you."

"I know," I said. "But they might."

"No," he said. "They won't."

He picked up his staff.

"You should probably get out," he said. "It's going to get dangerous."

Janice ran past me and slammed her bedroom door.

PAUL WOKE ME after midnight. He was wearing all black and had an *X* painted over his face. He was holding his staff.

"Come on," he said. "I need help."

"I have school in the morning," I said.

I rolled over. He rolled me back.

"Don't make me use this." He raised the staff over my head.

"Okay," I said. "But I'm not changing."

"Your loss," he said.

We climbed into Grandma's Cadillac. I was wearing boxers, flip-flops, and a Pippen jersey. Paul handed me the staff; I hugged it with my thighs.

We drove for ten minutes and pulled up in front of an apartment building. Paul turned off the car.

"Now," Paul said, "we wait."

"For what?" I asked.

"The prey," he said.

"I should be asleep," I said.

"You can sleep when you die," he said. "This is important."

Paul looked around.

"Never give up something without a fight," Paul said.

"I know," I said.

"How do you know?"

"You've told me that before," I said.

"Have I?" Paul asked.

"I think so," I said.

"Sounds like something I'd say."

"I know," I said.

"Raised you right," Paul said.

We both sat in silence and considered whether or not that was true.

"Do you ever talk to my parents?" I asked.

"I used to," he said. "When they first ran away."

"What are they like?" I asked.

"They're the same," he said. He didn't look at me. He kept his eyes on the deserted street. Whenever a car drove past, he ducked a little.

"I remember some things," I said.

"Like what?" Paul asked.

"Like Dad fighting that man in the street," I said.

Paul laughed.

"And Dad out in the lake when Jordan came back," I said.

"That did it for your mom," Paul said.

"What was Mom like?" I asked.

"Your mom wasn't like a mom," he said. "Your dad wasn't like a dad."

"What does that mean?" I asked.

"You were an accident," he said. "They never wanted you."

"I know that," I said. "Besides that."

"Duck," he said. "You're going to blow our cover."

I ducked.

"But what did they like?" I asked.

"Your dad liked poetry and Mike Royko," he said. "We all loved Mike Royko."

"I know about Mike Royko," I said.

We sat in silence and considered Mike Royko.

"Your mom liked thinking of better places," Paul said.

"When was the last time you talked to them?" I asked. The staff felt heavy between my legs.

"After the riots," he said. "They wanted to see if any of us died."

"Are they together?" I asked. "Are they happy?"

"They don't know what happiness is," he said. "They're not together."

"What do they do now?" I asked.

"Your mom is married to a man that makes boats," he said.

"Did she ask about me?" I asked.

"Of course," he said.

"What did you say?" I said.

"I said," Paul said, "you're fine without her."

"Does she ask about my life?" I asked.

"No," Paul said.

"Why?" I asked.

"She's selfish," Paul said.

Two adults on bicycles rode past, carried grocery bags on their handlebars, yelled about missing the bus.

"What does Dad do?" I asked.

"Duck lower," he said. "Go-time approaches."

"What does Dad do?" I asked again.

A gray truck crept past us.

"What?" he said. "Your dad is wandering, lost."

"Why?" I asked.

"Because he followed someone to Missouri," he said. "Don't follow people to Missouri."

The gray truck pulled into a spot up the block.

"It's go-time," Paul said. "Give me that."

Charles Doyle stepped out of the truck. He stood under a streetlight. He grabbed his bag from the backseat. He was wearing a janitor outfit. He hobbled in our direction.

"Keep a lookout," Paul said. His voice quivered.

He stepped out of the car with his staff. I rolled down my window. He jumped in front of the man and started wildly swinging. He held the staff out in front of his body. They advanced on each other.

"This is your last chance," Paul said. His legs were unstable.

"Round two?" Charles Doyle asked.

Paul got close enough to try a move I saw him practice on Grandma's mannequin. He jumped in the air, held the staff like a javelin, and tried to jab it into Charles Doyle's neck. He called it the kill shot. It worked one out of ten times against the mannequin. Charles Doyle stepped to the side. Paul lunged past him. Charles Doyle yanked the staff out of Paul's hands with ease. Paul turned around and sprinted back to the car. Charles Doyle was close behind.

"Start the car!" Paul yelled.

Lights turned on in the apartment building's windows.

A deep voice yelled out from above, "Paul! Paul!? I never loved you!"

I started the car. Paul slid over the hood. Charles Doyle broke a headlight with the staff. Paul crawled into the driver's seat, backed into the car behind us, set off the car's alarm, and tore down the street. Charles Doyle threw the staff. It pierced the rear window like a javelin.

"Come back for more!" Charles Doyle yelled.

Paul stopped the car, sniffled in the driver's seat, needed a minute, rubbed the steering wheel. I tapped his shoulder, once, twice.

"Paul," I said. "We gotta go."

I saw Charles Doyle in the rearview mirror, arms extended at his sides. Under the streetlight, his confused face looked orange and sick.

Paul accelerated down the empty street. He ran one red light. I told him to slow down. He stopped at an intersection and cried in deep heaves. He couldn't breathe, and snot shot from both nostrils. He sounded like a deflating mucus balloon. I rubbed his back, found a used and crusted tissue at my feet, offered it to him. He declined, wiped his fluids on his sleeve.

"I'm fine," Paul said. "This is life. I'm fine."

A car honked behind us. Paul drove home at a legal pace.

Janice was smoking on the porch when we pulled into the driveway. Paul tried to act smooth.

"Don't tell Grandma," he told us. He went inside. I stayed out with Janice.

"Can I go with you?" Janice asked. "To Missouri?"

I sat down next to her. I didn't notice my hands shaking in the car. I couldn't stop them.

"Paul almost got us killed," I said.

"I have nothing here," she said.

"What about the service industry?" I asked. "What about six figures? What about that guy?"

"He hasn't called me back," she said.

She put her head on my shoulder. She let her cigarette hang off her lips.

"What would you do there?" I asked.

"What will I do here?" she asked.

"I have to live in the dorms," I said.

"I'll live on the street," she said. "I need to get out of Chicago before I end up like everybody else."

"You're not like everybody else," I said.

"I'm cold," she said.

It wasn't cold. She kissed me on the cheek before she went up to her room.

The Cadillac looked worse in daylight. Grandma smashed plates in the kitchen. She cornered Paul. She called him names like clown and sorry boy. The staff was propped against the front door.

WHEN I GOT home from school, Janice told me about Amsterdam, Missouri. She came into my room holding an unfolded map of America.

"It's small," she said. "I need small right now."

"I have to live in Columbia," I said.

"Is Columbia small?" she asked.

"Not really," I said.

"I need small," she said.

"What's going on with you?" I asked.

She stood and placed the map on my carpet, rubbed it smooth with her feet and hands, rubbed her chin, seemed to look for something hidden in the charted highways and rivers.

"The world feels too big," she said.

"What if I stayed?" I asked.

"You have to leave," Janice said.

"Why?" I asked.

"You're not stupid," Janice said.

"You're not stupid either," I said.

"I know," Janice said.

"What do you want?" I asked.

"I want to live in Amsterdam with you," Janice said.

"Why?" I asked.

She stepped on the Midwest and Northeast, stepped on my toes, apologized, backed up.

"I want to start a bakery and you can write your stories," Janice said.

"You don't know how to bake," I said.

"I don't want children," Janice said.

"Me neither," I said.

"I just want to matter."

"You matter to me."

"And you're leaving."

Paul called for me.

"Claude!" he yelled. "Come check this out!"

Grandma yelled back. "No yelling! Everyone's on time-out!"

Janice followed me into Paul's room.

"Okay," he said. "So the staff was the problem."

"We shouldn't talk about this," I said.

"Okay," he said. "We need something lighter, something more aerodynamic."

"Like a knife," Janice said.

"I'm not trying to kill him," Paul said. "Just teach him a lesson. I'm too deadly with a knife."

Paul removed a pair of nunchaku from his desk drawer.

"Where did you get those?" I asked.

"I've been saving them for a special occasion," he said.

"He's going to kill you," I said.

"He is who will die," Paul said.

Paul took a wide stance, held his weapon above his head, closed his eyes, remained like that, taking slow and deep breaths.

"He's going to kill you," Janice said.

"It's too late to get in on the action, young lady," Paul said. "Your ship has sailed."

"Why do you care so much?" I asked.

"Because I have dignity," Paul said.

"No, you don't," Janice said.

"I have homework," I said.

Paul twirled the nunchaku, hit himself in the stomach. Janice left.

"You're going to kill yourself," I said.

"When someone wrongs you," he said, "they must pay for wronging you."

"It was just a man," I said.

"A man is never just a man," Paul said. "There are no small injustices in this world."

"Fine," I said. His eyes were tearing up.

"I need to practice," he said. "Get out. I will let you know when it's time."

Grandma was standing in my room.

"You know Paul is going to get himself killed, right?" she asked.

She sat on my bed and patted the spot next to her. I sat down and she inched closer to me.

"You know I didn't raise you like someone that follows their parents to Missouri," she said, "and follows idiots into street fights and gets their Grandma's Cadillac smashed up."

"Janice wants to come with me," I said.

"Are you guys fucking again?" she asked.

"No," I said.

"Is that why she's acting all crazy?" she asked.

"Why would that make her act crazy?" I asked.

"You're the best person in this house," she said. "That's not saying much. But it's saying something."

"What's it saying?" I asked.

"It's saying enough," she said. "This place is going to crumble without you."

She pinched my ear.

"The world might end."

She left.

"Give me those!" She yelled at Paul from down the hallway.

"This is an island of despair!" Paul yelled back.

"How much ass am I going to have to kick today?" Grandma sounded hollow. Like there was a part deep inside her that wasn't working right.

THAT NIGHT I thought about my parents. I looked into my mirror and imagined which features were Mom's, which were Dad's, and which belonged to some ancestor I'd never know about. I wondered what Mom sounded like when she wanted to kill Grandma. Did her voice sound like a cartoon's, like Janice's, or was it deep and forceful in a way that made you believe she could do it? I wondered if she possessed qualities that made her seem capable of anything and whether I got those qualities from her. Or did Grandma lie to me about my promise just to make me feel better, to make herself feel better about raising another failure?

I wondered whether Mom looked back at Chicago as she drove south, or was she moving too fast? I imagined her playing music I wouldn't recognize, windows down, throwing cigarette butts onto the prairie, burning fuel and rubber. I imagined her eyes forward, frozen on the road ahead.

Did she do things that made you love her no matter what, like Janice? Did she pull out her hair when she got nervous, or sneeze without covering her mouth and then apologize because her snot got everywhere, on everyone?

Dad I imagined in a motel, somewhere off an interstate, sweating in uncomfortable sleep, twisted in overused sheets. In my head, he sat on curbs, looked up, waited for cleansing rain, counted passing cars and buses. He was, in my head, always alone. I couldn't tell if those were tears of sadness or freedom.

Should I dream about them more? Should I fall asleep?

I fell asleep.

JANICE STOOD OVER my bed. It was still dark out. Her laptop screen illuminated her face. Her eyes were wild.

"There's a Paris in Missouri." She forced herself into bed next to me.

"What?" I said.

"It's bigger than Amsterdam," she said. "But it's still small."

"I don't know," I said.

"Fine," she said. "There's a Mexico."

"Why don't you just go to the real Mexico?" I asked.

"You wouldn't be there," she said. "And I don't have a passport."

She put her computer down and spooned against me. Her head was in my armpit. Her hair smelled like smoke. We slept like that.

Grandma woke us up.

"Sorry Boy is in the hospital."

PAUL HAD TRIED round three with Charles Doyle. This time he took his nunchaku. He thought if he exercised some control and precision Charles Doyle would live. Charles Doyle took the nunchaku from Paul. Paul tripped and fell on broken glass. His stomach got cut up. Charles Doyle drove him to the hospital in Grandma's Cadillac. He didn't want to get blood in his truck. We had to take a cab to the hospital.

Charles Doyle was at the hospital talking to the cops. He didn't recognize me. He didn't want to press charges. He thought Paul had learned his lesson.

"It's sad," Charles Doyle told the cops. "He thought he was dying. He said everything he loved was going to Missouri. I think he pissed himself."

AT GRADUATION, PAUL handled the video camera. An alumna—a painter—gave the commencement address. She said life was hard and gets harder. She thanked her friends and family. Without them, she said, she would've committed suicide by jumping off a medium-size apartment complex. "Go forth," she said. "Make waves." Grandma gave a standing ovation, cupped her hands around her mouth and hollered.

I tripped when they called my name, grabbed my diploma, put my sweating hand into the principal's, and tripped off the stage.

Janice had a bouquet for me, wilted tulips. Paul's crying ripped open his stiches. He bled through his suit. He forgot to turn on the camera.

"My little man," Paul sniffled. "Little, little man."

Grandma let him rest against her.

We walked home in a solemn procession, ordered pizza.

JANICE AND I went out onto the porch after dinner.

"I'm not coming with you," Janice said.

"I figured," I said.

"It was a stupid idea," Janice said.

"I know," I said.

"I'm not like you," Janice said. "I can't leave."

"Sure you can," I said.

"Fine," Janice said. "I won't leave. I don't want to leave. Missouri sounds horrible."

"What are you going to do?" I asked.

"This guy got me a job downtown," Janice said.

"Six figures?" I asked.

"I'm too young to serve liquor," Janice said. "They call it hostessing?"

"A hostess?" I asked.

"Yeah," Janice said. "At this club."

"Are you happy?" I asked.

"Are you happy?" Janice asked.

"I might be," I said.

"You want to know what I think?" Janice asked.

"Sure," I said.

"I think happiness is an illusion," Janice said. "Are you making your own decisions? Are you taking your own chances? Are your failures worth it? Do you make dynamite?"

"What?" I asked.

"We'll be okay," Janice said.

Two days later, Janice was gone. She moved into a studio apartment up north. She filled her duffle bag with wrinkled dresses. Her club was called Barcelona.

Sunset

//////////////////////////

PAUL SAID TO look scary so people wouldn't sit next to me. We were standing downtown waiting for the Megabus. To our right a man in a wrinkled blue suit crouched down and hugged two children. He was crying. The children were too. A woman stood behind the children; her arms were crossed and she was tapping her foot. After a few moments she pulled the kids away. She turned her head when the man in the wrinkled blue suit tried to kiss her forehead. The woman and children left, disappeared behind an office building. The bus was already fifteen minutes late. I only had a duffle bag. Paul and Grandma were going to mail me everything else. Microwave, Emmett Till poster, waffles, toaster, et cetera.

"At least you're not like that guy," Paul said, loudly enough for the man in the wrinkled blue suit to hear.

Paul had spent the whole morning trying to cheer me up. I told him I wasn't sad, which was true. He insisted I was in denial. Grandma couldn't bear my leaving. She protested, was still in bed when I left. After I bent down and kissed her forehead, she rolled over, pulled the sheet up to her nose, turned her back on me. I heard "I love you" when I closed the door. Or "Fuck you."

The ground shook my feet.

"Here it comes," Paul said.

The Megabus driver slammed on the brakes. He hopped out. He was wide-eyed and shaking.

"Let's do this," he said. "Let's take y'all to another planet."

"It's not too late," Paul said as he hoisted my duffle bag in next to the other luggage. It was too late. He wasn't crying. I could tell he was trying his best not to. He probably thought his crying would make me cry. It wouldn't have.

"Remember," he said, "fart or burp if someone tries to sit next to you."

He didn't stay after I got on. He crossed the street and disappeared.

I-55 TAKES YOU from Chicago to Missouri, takes you through parts of Chicago I forgot existed: the Mexican neighborhoods that were once Polish neighborhoods, the Polish neighborhoods that were once swampland, the large chain auto parts shops that were once mom and pop auto parts shops. You have to take I-55 to get to Brookfield Zoo. Brookfield was out in the suburbs. I heard that zoo was nicer than ours.

I-55 ended in St. Louis. Almost everybody got off in St. Louis. We got on I-70, which cut straight westward through the gut of Missouri. The bus drove into the sunset. In Chicago, I'd never seen a sunset. The buildings blocked the sun as it dipped below the horizon.

Interlude

////////////////////////////

OUTSIDE SPRINGFIELD, a giant neon horseshoe sparkled over us and the gas station. We had twenty minutes to do whatever we had to do: eat, smoke, go to the bathroom, sit and watch the cars pass on the highway, sit and look out into the flatness.

I saw two bus stations that day, hundreds of miles apart, similar in almost every way except in noise and bustle. Here: a short man cried atop a pile of luggage, under a faded streetlight; all the streetlights were faded, illuminated soft scenes.

I wanted to tell Janice about the boring things I saw. I wanted to hear about her new job. I could hear her voice clearly—swearing, sweet—echoing in my head. I tried to call. She didn't pick up. I didn't leave a message.

I used the urinal between two wide men wearing Cardinals jerseys. They spat dip into their piss. They gave me sideways glances. I couldn't go.

Outside, I tried to call Janice again. The bus driver yelled and honked as I tried to leave a message.

PART TWO

///////////////////////////////

Missouri

Icebreaker

////////////////////////////////////

RA TOM ESCORTED us, our entire floor, into the common room. He asked the sleeping person on our common couch if he lived here. The person said no without opening his eyes. RA Tom told the person to please leave. We all stood there while the person walked out without opening his eyes. We stood there until he disappeared into an elevator and was never seen again, at least, not on our floor.

"Great!" RA Tom slapped his hands against his cargo shorts.

We had to sit in a circle, legs crossed, name tags visible. Some of the sad-looking kids chose to lean against the wall with their feet barely in the circle. Some of the kids with piercings wrote crude nicknames on their name tags. Prince Dick, for example.

I sat next to my roommate, Kenneth. He smelled like dust. Pimple scars ran from his ears down to his chin. He had short, sharp hair like broken spaghetti.

We had to say three things: name, hometown, major. If we were feeling adventurous and open—"No pressure," RA Tom added, "only if you want to"—you could say what animal you'd choose as a partner for the apocalypse.

"I'll go first," RA Tom said. His dress shirt looked too big for him, even with the sleeves rolled up and the bottom tucked into his cargo shorts. He didn't pull off his look: the spiked blond hair and flip-flops and ankle bracelet. His face was too formless, his eyes, too black.

"My name is Tom . . . Oh, when you say your name, we'll all say 'Hey, blank!' My name's Tom."

"Hey, Tom."

"I'm from Kirkwood. My major is agriculture with an emphasis on animal husbandry. And, let's see, animal, animal, animal. Oh! A cow. A strong and loyal cow. Okay. Next."

"Hey. My name's Molly."

"Hey, Molly."

"I'm also from Kirkwood. Funny. Um, my major is biology. I think. I might switch. I'll probably switch. I don't know."

We were bored after Molly, after RA Tom, really. We were bored and agitated after Bradley, Jayson with a *Y*, Samantha, Justin G., Justin S., Justin Q., Samuel, Bertha, Justine, David B. from Kansas City, David B. from St. Louis—we were ready to lose it.

"I'm Claude."

"Hey."

"Where are you from, Claude?"

"Chicago. Sorry."

"Like D Rose?"

"Like Chief Keef?"

"Like Obama?"

"You're like Obama."

"You know Chief Keef?"

"You're just like Obama."

"And that's it! Thanks for bringing us home, Claude!"

The Prairie Executioner

WHITNEY TORE MY second draft to shreds, right in my face, right on my lap, and kicked over a tiny garbage can; Whitney was disgusted. Her brown hair, frizzed in the humidity, created a wild frame around her sunburned face. She had just gotten back from a Caribbean island, and her pale skin was red and peeling around her shoulders.

Whitney sat on my desk, looked at my shredded 250 words on the volleyball team's bake sale, drummed a pencil on her lap—What are we going to do with you, Claude?

"How are you adjusting, Claude?" Whitney asked.

"I'm good," I said. "I just need to use the bathroom."

My desk was the type of desk you found in classrooms, a seat with a plastic slab raised over the lap. Whitney was small enough to sit on the plastic slab without the plastic slab moaning, the only person small enough; other people wouldn't dare. You didn't want to stick out for the wrong reasons: breaking a desk, burning toast, deleting the front page, spelling Tennyson with an *i*, spilling hot coffee on your shirt, spilling hot coffee on your pants, screaming at hot coffee soaking through your jeans, showing up late, showing up on the wrong day, showing up when no one needed you, not being needed. Two months in and I stuck out. Other editors and reporters listened to Whitney while she drummed her pencil and sucked her teeth. Typing slowed down; conversations turned to murmurs.

"Look," Whitney said. "No one is a natural. This is an unnatural enterprise, getting in people's business."

You also didn't want to cry. Not in the newsroom.

"I have to go to the bathroom," I said.

"Go," Whitney said. "Come back and finish."

She got off my desk and my desk didn't make a sound. Before she disappeared behind a row of filing cabinets, she gave me the same thumbs up and frown she had given me every day.

The *Prairie Executioner* claimed the oldest history of any student newspaper in the Union or Confederacy. "Fuck the *Crimson*, Harvard fucks" was chiseled into the kitchenette tiles. We Keep Them Honest was the official motto underneath the masthead. The newsroom was beneath Mark Twain Hall, in a basement with little else—unisex bathroom, boiler room, separate office for the editor-in-chief, two broken vending machines. The *Prairie Executioner* once had its own building. That was before the Civil War broke out and Confederate sympathizers burned down the newsroom. The *Prairie Executioner* claimed the first abolitionist editorial stance west of the Mississippi.

I wiped my eyes and blew my nose and called Janice.

"You again?" she asked. She was on a boat. I could hear the waves and the sliding champagne glasses.

"I don't think I can do this," I said.

"You keep fucking up," she said. "Nothing wrong with fucking up."

"I miss you," I said.

"You keep saying that," she said, "and I'm going to start believing you."

She hung up after a loud horn sounded somewhere across the water.

I stared at my phone, hoped she hung up and forgot about me by accident. After a few minutes, I went back to the newsroom.

All new reporters had a desk like mine; editors were across the room in a row of cubicles, ten of them, seniors with columns and internships lined up. In between the editors and reporters: the Pit.

The Pit was a twenty-foot snakewood table crowded with chairs; second- and third-year reporters shared the Pit. When I got back, Whitney was on the table telling everyone to gather around and shut the hell up. Whitney made all her announcements from atop the Pit. She extended her arms, made herself big, stirred fear into the tension.

"Feeding time!" Whitney yelled, like she always yelled before the afternoon meetings. Whitney started with the editors.

"Peanut," Whitney said. "Sports?"

"Soccer, good to go. Volleyball and cross country, good to go by five."

"Bowtie," Whitney said. "Art?"

"Fauvist exhibit is coming down this week. I think sculptures, Rodin-like, are coming next."

"'Think'? 'Like'? Specific, specific."

Whitney pointed at you with rolled-up papers after calling your name. She would extend her arm, unmoving, until you satisfied her question. She held her fencer's pose as Bowtie wiped sweat from his nose.

"Rummy," Whitney said. "Politics?"

"Greek life elections are next month. Should be close."

"Pudding Snack," Whitney said. "Fashion?"

"Fur boots column is 90 percent there."

"Carload," Whitney said.

A slamming door cut Whitney off.

I had heard of Connie Stove before that moment. She once drank Tom Brokaw under the table. She was at Kent State in 1970; she was in Berlin when the wall came down. Her gray hair was starting to turn baby blue.

Whitney stood at attention, like a sergeant or enforcer. Word had it the *Times* gave Connie Stove the boot after she called Arthur Sulzberger Jr. a pig with no morals, no better than the other pigs. The university wrote her a check, and there she was: faculty advisor and editor-in-chief of the *Prairie Executioner*.

"Please," Connie Stove said, "continue."

Whitney appeared to bow. Her neck compressed. Her shoulders dipped.

"Carload!" Whitney puffed her chest out and lunged toward Carload. "Football."

"We've got five reporters at practice today, tomorrow, and Friday. Sit-downs with Coach Smoke tomorrow and Friday. Sit-down with John-Michael Jeremy on Friday. Three reporters at the game on Saturday. Six reporters hitting tailgates on Saturday. We'll be ready to run Sunday night."

Football writers, much like the players and coaches they covered, operated under mysterious regulations. Whitney never threatened to bite off a football writer's ears.

"Excellent," Whitney said.

She continued down the list:

Chocolate Chip, National: column rating Barack's reaction to gun violence and recent shootings, almost done, waiting for fact checkers.

Roses, Crime: reporters at the station trying to figure out what happened in Greek City, the victim won't press charges; reporters checking on the recent break-ins on Red Campus; researching crime from Chicago and St. Louis spilling into the area, another shooting last night.

Pampers, Entertainment: new Coen Brothers review good to go; *Where the Wild Things Are* is out next week; Missouri Theatre is getting ready to close, feature on that will be ready at the end of the month.

Cherry, Weather and Agriculture: corn harvest is coming in slow; global warming spread should be finished in two months.

Whitney, Editorial: continued series on diversity on campus, this time it's a letter from an alumna; they found another burial ground during construction, slaves this time.

"Back at it!" Whitney hopped off the desk.

"Please," Connie Stove said, "sit down, everybody."

Whitney moved closer to Connie Stove and sat cross-legged next to a dried puddle of spilled soda.

"You may be hearing a lot of talk about our current state of affairs." Connie Stove craned her neck as she spoke, to look each person in the face, even downward for Whitney. She moved and spoke at a patient and comforting pace. During her speech, we made eye contact four times. Twice, I blinked. Once, I looked away. Finally, I held it and saw only dead puddles reflecting back.

"Our current state of affairs, that is, us, this thing we do, have to do—our fucking jobs. Does anyone know why I'm here? I was getting Walter Cronkite coffee when JFK got his head blown off. I once smuggled myself into West Germany to have tea with a triple agent. So why am I here? Readership is down. Quality across the country is down. Papers are cutting investigative teams left and right. Why am I here? I used to go sailing with Helen Thomas off the coast of Maine, cold water, then grab some lobsters; you could get fresh butter from the source back then. They say the field is dying. Online this, online that. They said the same thing about the radio and the television and the microwave. They said the same thing about me. I once got slapped in the face and the ass for missing a deadline. I stabbed that man with a letter opener and left him bleeding in the stairwell. I loved my first husband. He hated this world. Do you know what a light bulb overheating and popping sounds like? Do you know what it's like to follow that sound into the garage and see the only person you ever wanted to see, slumped over their gut, that gut you complained about over the years, since you got married, since you worked to keep your body slim for the newsroom, since you did everything for the newsroom, the newsroom stood for something, and you forgot the past four anniversaries—that kind of thing makes you question."

Connie Stove pushed back from the Pit and exited into her office.

"Dismissed," Whitney said.

ON FRIDAY, WHEN everybody was packing up, Whitney wanted to talk to the black reporters, the only black people on staff, about a new diversity project. There was me and one more: Simone.

"I still have the volleyball story," I said.

"Don't talk," Whitney said. "Connie wants you two to work on this."

"That's messed up," Simone said.

Simone grew up outside Kansas City in a house with a barn in the backyard. She smoked two packs a day and chewed three packets of gum; sometimes her cigarettes were light, sometimes her gum was strawberry. I heard her dad was Dutch or Ukrainian.

"I know," Whitney said. "Don't talk."

"What do we have to do?" I asked.

Whitney looked at me the same way then as she did when, on my first day, I dropped a full plate of mashed potatoes and gravy on her backpack.

"Come back next week with ideas," Whitney said. "This, now—this is your life."

"Ideas about what?" I asked.

"Get out," Whitney said.

Whitney put her head on her desk when we had turned around and she thought we wouldn't look back.

Simone and I left the office together, for the first time.

There was a light on in Connie Stove's office, a soft and orange light from underneath the windowless door. A single voice came out too; it sounded like a person talking to a mirror.

"What kind of ideas should we think of?" I asked when we got outside.

"This smells like bullshit," Simone said while digging around in her bag. Cigarettes, reds, blue lighter, small flame, a few tries—smoke.

"Maybe it'll be good for our careers," I said, looking at Simone.

Her purple fingernails were bitten to the meat.

"Can I bum a square?" I said.

"Square?" Simone said.

"A cig," I whispered.

"What's a square?" Simone asked.

"Guess it's a Chicago thing," I said.

"Cool," Simone said.

"Walking this way?" I asked.

"Sure," Simone said.

Simone lived in the Meredith Miles Marmaduke Mansion, a house for special scholarship students. She thought I was surprised at her intelligence. She said people were often surprised at her intelligence, and it made her want to choke and bite and elbow. I wasn't surprised. I was disappointed that she lived so close to the office. She left me at the bottom of the staircase. She walked on the balls of her feet. She bounced.

"You know," Simone said, without turning around, "this is bullshit."

When she disappeared inside, I stopped thinking about Simone. I started thinking about Janice. I heard her voice on the walk back to my dorm, in the breeze. I turned around and wanted to find her hiding behind a tree, trying to scare me, playing a game. She wasn't there. She was far away.

KENNETH WAS BUILDING a blanket fort, poorly, when I got back. He couldn't figure out the mechanics of it. He wanted to smoke inside without setting off the fire alarm. I walked in, and he had a pillow under one arm and a chair under the other, looking at his bed, looking at the floor, looking at the ceiling.

"I have some work to do," I said.

"Me too," he said, still entranced or depressed.

I sat on my bed and thought up ideas.

More breakfast options.

Fewer fried options at lunch and dinner.

Where does the chicken come from?

Is our corn local?

Why don't all cooks have to wear hairnets?

Less security at dining halls.

Fried ravioli vs. Bosco sticks.

Why is there ranch on everything?

Why does everyone put ranch on everything?

Frank's hot sauce is only good on Buffalo wings.

Why are all the fast food options burger places?

The broccoli is rubbery.

Where do you get rubbery broccoli?

Where does it end?

Does it go all the way to the top?

Will we ever know?

Kenneth struggled to tape his sheet to the ceiling. I offered to help. The tape was weak; the sheet, heavy.

I had learned not to question his motivations. There was a thunderstorm in Kenneth's head. Once, I asked what a water-filled trash can was doing in his closet. He said it was for catfish. I asked why he needed catfish in his closet. For an hour, he told me about Wal-Mart, the destroyed middle class, warming oceans and rivers, nuclear waste, and the agriculture-industrial complex.

I decided not to ask about the fort, or anything else.

"Another day," Kenneth said when we gave up.

Routine

////////////////////////////

IF YOU SHOWERED in the morning, more piss splashed around your feet. If you showered at night—that's when the moaning started, soft and lonely whimpers filled with longing, unromantic in their steadiness, a pounding and mechanical rhythm, efficient and solitary.

If you showered at night, you might hear an old girlfriend's name. You might hear two recent boyfriends experimenting for the first time, trying it out, seeing how it fits and feels.

Once, I heard David B. from Kansas City convince David B. from St. Louis that he felt love when they held each other. I was brushing my teeth. They were in the stall farthest from the door. All that running water made it feel like we were under a waterfall, in a movie, right before happily ever after. Someone across the room, in the toilet stall closest to the door, started humming *The Wonder Years* theme song.

Justin S. screamed into his loofah every night. He was violent with himself. He'd call on Aphrodite to release his lurid cravings, to free him from desire. Justin S. wore flip-flops with baby sparrows on them. His showers lasted over an hour. I went back to my room if I saw him coming up the hall in his robe and carrying his wicker basket filled with generic cleaners and scrubbers for his temperamental skin.

I met a woman in there one Thursday afternoon. She had a bladder emergency and didn't know this was the men's room: Sorry, sorry, excuse me. Wait—how do you get piss on the ceiling? Why is the floor sticky?

I peeked out my curtain and shrugged at her. She did not seem at ease. She whispered private words to herself and went into a toilet stall.

If you showered in the afternoon, you weren't a part of something larger. You just wanted to get clean and masturbate in peace.

Sociology #1

///

"SOCIOLOGY," PROFESSOR JANUS said the first day. "Sociology is about trees in a forest."

Professor Janus wanted our class to call him Professor Jim, for short, for friendliness, relaxation, and comfort. No one wanted to call him Professor Jim. No one did. Professor Janus wanted to play a game: write your hometown on a piece of paper and write five things that make your hometown special; note similarities, note differences, notice how small the world is, notice humanity.

"Okay," Professor Janus said. "Who wants to go first? Wait, first, say your hometown, and then say two things from your list. Got it? Okay. Who wants to go first?"

Professor Janus pointed to someone in the first row. I couldn't see from way in the back. The person sounded tired and annoyed, like everyone felt.

"I'm from Joplin. Langston Hughes is from Joplin. Our homecoming had a real tiger, from India."

"Okay," Professor Janus said. "Joplin. Great. Who's next?"

"I'm from the Hill. Italian food, stuff like that. I'm Italian. Baseball."

"I'm from Joplin. Hey, Laura. We went to high school together. Yeah. Langston Hughes is from there."

"I'm from Topeka. *Brown v. Board.* The capital. That's about it."

"I'm from Washington. Meth labs. Meth heads. Meth dealers. I hate it. It doesn't taste good. It fucks your skin up. That whole town smells like melted plastic and poison flowers."

"I'm from Carthage. Joplin sucks."

"You suck."

"We beat Joplin in basketball four years in a row."

"We beat Carthage in football."

"Carthage doesn't matter."

"Nothing matters."

"This whole state is just fields for dying corn."

"And meth labs."

"And meth labs, yeah."

"Nothing interesting happens here."

"I'm from Pennsylvania."

"Pennsylvania sucks too."

"Yeah, I know."

"Whoa. Wait. Stan Musial is from Pennsylvania."

"Stan the Man."

"Pennsylvania doesn't suck too bad."

"Hershey's chocolate."

"August Wilson."

"I'm from Kansas City."

"Royals suck."

"Yeah, Royals suck."

"Royals suck, yeah."

"Do you remember a time when the Royals didn't suck and Kansas wasn't just an overflowing toilet?"

I looked down at my list, chewed my eraser, rehearsed my answer: Chicago, South Shore, President Obama lived near there, the riot, basketball, mustard, Italian beef and sausage.

"Okay," Professor Janus said. "Great. Okay. Well, that's it for today—we'll finish tomorrow. Oh! Please bring your list back on Wednesday."

Five minutes to the hour, when most classes ended, a pulsing student swarm took over campus. I rode the swarm to the journalism office, listened to conversation snippets. I wondered how so many people could have nothing interesting to say. I missed the conversations I overheard back home, on the bus, walking down Sixty-Seventh, on the couch with Paul and Grandma. Here, in the swarm, two guys in backward trucker hats talked about drinking thirty beers each and throwing up in a river. Another guy, on the phone, said he couldn't talk about hazing rituals, Mom. A young professor carried overflowing manila folders with both arms, pushed through, groaned when students wouldn't walk faster, make way. Somewhere up ahead, someone screamed in joy. Another scream followed.

Whitney and Simone were talking in the hall when I walked down the stairs.

"Claude," Whitney said. "Good. You're here."

"She's making us stay late," Simone said to me, still looking at Whitney.

"Is that a problem?" Whitney asked.

"What if I have class?" Simone asked.

"Do you?" Whitney asked.

"That's not the point," Simone said.

"Fill him in," Whitney said, and walked into the office.

Simone put palms over her eyes, bent over, groaned, slid to the ground, looked up at me.

"So," I said. "What's up?"

Simone held up her finger, asked for a minute, gathered herself, stood, brushed herself off.

"We have to research," Simone said.

"Research what?" I asked.

"Come on." Simone opened the office door. "I'll show you."

Simone showed me a backroom at the office's far end. The backroom's door was covered in bumper stickers from all over the world, layered, faded, peeling, crusted. Simone had the key to get in.

Inside, two new-looking computers sat on a graffitied fold-out table. In front of each computer was a new-looking rolling chair. The walls were penciled and penned over to the point where all the messages were almost indecipherable. Staring into the wall was staring into swirling chaos. Someone had written

"I LUV YOU" above "I HATE THIS PLACE." Most of the scribbles were swear words and slang for sex and getting high.

"What the fuck?" I asked the room.

"We have to stay here," Simone said.

"And research," Whitney said to our backs.

"It's dark," I said.

"It smells," Simone said.

"The light's here," Whitney said, without pointing to a light switch. "You're gonna wanna close the door."

"Why?" Simone asked.

"Connie's coming," Whitney said, "and she's going to yell."

The door closed us in darkness. The tight space vibrated at a low frequency—it was hard to breathe.

After some fumbling, awkward touching, accidental groping, apologies, we found the light switch.

"Alright," Simone said. "Let's get started."

Inside the computers were every issue of the *Prairie Executioner*, digitized, stacked in organized folders by year and month, arranged in columns and rows on the desktop. Our task: look through and find articles about race on campus.

"Look through all this?" I said.

"That's what she wants," Simone said, scrolling and clicking already.

"Why?" I asked.

"Research," Simone said. "Background. Our project, you know."

"We have to look at every issue?" I said.

Simone sighed, stopped scrolling and clicking.

"Start with familiar dates," Simone said. "Start with historic dates."

"What are historic dates?" I asked.

Simone rolled her eyes, sucked her teeth, pulled a notebook from her backpack.

"When was Martin Luther King killed?" Simone asked.

"Nineteen sixty-eight," I said, remembered Paul and Grandma.

"Right," Simone said. "In April. Now, look in April 1968 and see what campus was like."

"Right," I said.

"Except," Simone said, "I'm looking at April 1968. You look at something else."

Simone looked at the screen, wrote something down, looked back at the screen, wrote something else down, put earbuds in, played her music too loud, something with bass and yelling.

I took out my notebook and pen; I tried to remember my history classes and stories I had overheard back home.

Brown v. Board: *1954.*

Red Summer: 1919.

Harlem Renaissance: 1920s.

Voting Rights Act: 1965.

Rodney King Riots: 1992.

Emancipation: 1865.

I tapped my pen against my notebook, forehead, thigh, and tongue; I couldn't remember more; I didn't know where to start.

"Hey." I tapped my pen against Simone's shoulders.

She pulled one earbud out, didn't look away from her screen.

"What now?"

"Are all your dates about bad stuff?"

"What do you mean?"

"I have this list. And it's all about death and fixing injustice."

"So?"

"Just saying."

She put her earbud back in, turned her music up.

I started backward, opened the folder from November 2008, almost a year ago: Election Day.

There, staring and smiling, dusted with fallen confetti, Obama waved at the camera. Balloons too, captured floating in midair. The headline, big and bold, wide and tall: OBAMA MAKES HISTORY. I remembered watching Obama and Michelle and Sasha and Malia walk on stage. Janice went up to the Grant Park viewing party with a lawyer acquaintance. Next to me, Paul and Grandma wiped tears away; laughed at Jesse Jackson crying; cheered at Oprah, in the front row, crying too, smiling, nodding her head. Grandma and Paul spoke to the television.

"Go 'head."

"There he go."

"Here he goes."

"There he goes."

"We'll never see him again."

"Do you, baby."

"Go 'head."

Grandma changed the channel before Obama spoke, wiped more tears from her eyes, couldn't speak. Paul put an arm around her.

"God damn," Grandma said.

"Damn," Paul said.

"He did it," Grandma said.

Paul took the remote from Grandma, flipped back to Obama, mid-sentence, arms outstretched.

"What if he forgets us?" Grandma asked the television.

"It won't matter," Paul said. "That's our boy."

"That's our boy," Grandma repeated.

Without realizing it, I was crying streams, and snot ran over my lips, stuck to my chin. I excused myself, went to the bathroom, cried some more, wiped my entire face. Through the door, from the living room, Grandma and Paul screamed.

"That's my boy!"

"That's my motherfucking boy!"

"There he goes."

"Go 'head."

"Go motherfucking 'head."

Without realizing it, sitting next to Simone, staring at a digitized Obama, my eyes leaked. I hoped she hadn't noticed. If she had, she didn't want me to know. She kept her head straight, scrolled, clicked, jotted down notes. I wiped my eyes, kept scrolling and clicking through history. Back then, on election night, I didn't think much of those tears, just thought they were a reflex. Now, they felt powerful. I made a note that election night still made me cry.

I lost track of time, found myself floating between decades, lingered when something caught my attention. In 1986, a black high school basketball star was caught with cocaine in his car,

suspended, then expelled, and sent to Boone County Jail where he hanged himself in his cell. I noted that. His name was ——
——, an invisible man.

In 1995, City Council held an urgent meeting to discuss gangsta rap. That's it. They just wanted to discuss gangsta rap and how horrible it sounded. They played 2 Live Crew in the chambers, aghast.

In 1979, two cops beat a homeless black man to death. No reason was given. No charges were brought. They didn't give his name.

In 1943, two cops arrested a black veteran for trying to enter the all-white American Legion. According to the reporter, the Negro made a scene, refused to leave, shouted about his sacrifices and human rights. The cops beat the Negro. They didn't give his name.

In 1863, two professors debated whether abolition was worth all these valuable white lives. Both sides agreed it wasn't. They disagreed on whether the Confederacy should remain in the Union or secede, once a truce was reached and President Lincoln got off his moral high horse. They made reference to unnamed freed niggers, loitering about town, committing small crimes, and scaring good whites, promoting unrest. The article was a direct contradiction of the *Prairie Executioner*'s self-written history.

I needed a break.

"Hey," I said to Simone.

She didn't hear me.

I tapped her shoulder; she pulled out an earbud, kept staring at the screen.

"This is depressing," I said. "I'm going to get some air."

Simone nodded, put her earbud back in.

I put my notebook away, turned the computer off, picked up my bag, looked over Simone's shoulder before I opened the door. On her screen: black people hanging from thick tree branches, a white crowd gathered.

"Where are you going?" Whitney asked as I walked past her desk.

"I need some air," I said.

"What does that mean?" Whitney asked.

I didn't have time to answer. Connie Stove slammed into the room.

"Okay!" Connie Stove yelled. "Shut up!"

I slid behind her, up the stairs, out the door, into a quiet campus—classes still in session. I stood in the sun for a moment, fought back tears I didn't expect. My head rattled with noise and anger. I wanted home. I headed for my dorm, tried to hide my eyes from passersby.

Reunion

///////////////////////////

WHEN I GOT back from the office, I heard voices behind my door. I put my ear against the thin wood. If Kenneth was with a guest, I didn't want to disturb. I heard him discussing the finer points of street-sign theft. I heard the other voice mumble along, disinterested and half-hearted. I took my chances.

Janice.

Janice was cross-legged on my bed with her back against the wall. There was a duffel bag next to her. Her loose sweater exposed her left shoulder, the shoulder closest to me. She had a red streak in her straightened hair. She looked up when I walked in. She tucked loose hair strands behind her ear. Her face was thinner than I remembered. Her smile was the same.

"You didn't tell me you had a sister," Kenneth said twice before I heard him.

"She's not my sister," I said.

"Sort of," Janice said to Kenneth. "In a way."

"Kenneth," I said.

"You want me to leave?" Kenneth asked.

"Please," I said.

"He's a loser," Janice said when Kenneth closed the door.

"He's nice," I said.

"He's worse than you." Janice grinned.

"What does that mean?" I asked.

"Were you crying?"

"No."

"This place made you soft."

I sat on the floor. She draped her feet over the bed, dangled them in my face. I took one of her ankles in my left hand, wrapped my fingers all around.

"Everything okay?" I asked.

"Why do you ask?" Janice asked.

"Because you're here," I said, "in my dorm room, in my bed, in Missouri."

"I can't visit?" Janice asked.

I couldn't see her face from my position. She jerked her feet when she spoke.

"We haven't spoken in weeks," I said.

"Months," Janice said. "Maybe."

"When was the last time I saw you?" I asked.

"It doesn't matter," Janice said.

"What are you going to do?" I said.

"Eat," Janice said. "I'm hungry."

She jumped off the bed, almost stomped on my gut. She hoisted me up.

"I have homework," I said.

"I want tacos," Janice said.

She put her head into my chest. I wrapped my arms around her. She tucked her hands into her pockets.

"You can talk to me," I said.

She looked up, for a moment, with unmistakable sadness and fear. Then she smiled, tapped my ribs with her fist, poked my shin with her shoes, and pulled me toward the door.

"Not now," Janice said. "Not yet."

"There's a place downtown," I said.

"Hold up," Janice said.

She pulled a few twenties from her pocket.

"What's that?" I asked.

"My treat," Janice said.

As we walked down Main Road, from campus to downtown, Janice turned heads. Girlfriends punched their boyfriends who were staring too long. Cars hung up traffic when red lights turned green. A police officer stopped scribbling a ticket. Everyone saw what I saw: someone who didn't belong, a person steps above us. She didn't seem to notice the stares, or notice anything. She kept her head down. I tried to ask her questions, and she deflected with grunts and shrugs. I stuck my hand across her chest to keep her from oncoming traffic. She grunted thanks and kept moving, without looking.

Her phone kept ringing. And she kept hanging up.

Martin's Taco Palace was a thin hole in the wall flanked by a new frozen yogurt place and a new smoothie spot. You could walk past Martin's without noticing it, like we did, twice. Downtown was trying to change, prosper, evolve, and catch up. Places like Martin's were remnants of a psychedelic past. All college towns, I heard, embraced the seventies more than any other decade. Most were able to shrug it off when the new millennium hit. Not Martin's. There were glow-in-the-dark peace signs stuck to the ceiling. Faded posters of Joan Baez, Joni Mitchell, and Jimi Hendrix hung over the booths. Martin's was 80 percent booths. A small open kitchen was beyond the counter. Martin sat on the counter, gray hair spooling down his torso into his lap. We were the only patrons.

"A romantic lunch?" Martin asked us when we entered.

"Sure," Janice said, removed from her trance. "Why not?"

Martin slid off the counter, grabbed a few menus, and beckoned us to follow him toward Jimi Hendrix's booth.

We sat down and Martin hovered over us, frozen and, it seemed, broken. His face turned blank, drool gathered on his lip. I coughed. Martin came back to us.

"Today's special," Martin said. "Crayfish enchiladas."

"Can we have some water?" I asked.

"Time for my smoke," Martin said.

Martin shuffled through the kitchen and out the back door.

"Do you eat here every day?" Janice asked.

"This is my first time," I said.

"Looks like a shithole," Janice said.

"I'm sorry," I said. "We can go somewhere else."

"I like shitholes," Janice said.

I wanted her to tell me everything all at once. Why was she here? Why didn't she call before she came? Who was calling her now? Why did she look defeated? Did she need help? I started with the most immediate concern.

"What do you want to eat?" I asked.

"These pork tacos look good," Janice said.

"What are you doing here?" I asked.

"Or," Janice said, "the chipotle chicken."

"Janice," I said in a voice I hoped carried concern and love.

"I don't want to talk about it," Janice said.

"What are you going to do?" I asked.

"First," Janice said, "I'm going to eat."

"You can't stay in my dorm room," I said.

"Your roommate might kill people for fun," Janice said.

"I know," I said.

"Can we talk about something else?" Janice asked.

"Like what?" I asked.

"Like you," Janice said. "How are you doing?"

"I don't know," I said.

"How can you not know?" Janice said.

"I've only been here a couple months," I said.

"That's long enough," Janice said.

"I hate it," I said.

"That's what I thought."

"How?"

"I know you," Janice said.

"And I know you," I said.

Janice looked back at her menu, turned it over a few times, looked for something else to talk about. She turned it faster and faster until she slammed it on the table. Martin appeared, a weed-perfumed apparition.

"Ready to order?" Martin asked.

"No," I said.

"Yes," Janice said. "He'll have the crayfish enchiladas; I'll take the crazy potato tacos."

Martin took our menus. Janice grabbed his tie-dyed shirt as he walked away.

"Our waters?" Janice asked.

"Water don't work," Martin said. His eyes were hot red and sweating.

"What are we supposed to drink?" Janice asked.

"Our margaritas come with lime wedges," Martin said.

"We'll take two margaritas," Janice said.

"Coming up," Martin said. "After my smoke break."

Martin disappeared, again, out the back door. I understood, at that moment, our chances at a meal were slim to none.

"Does Grandma know you're here?" I asked.

"She doesn't care," Janice said.

"She does," I said.

"I haven't been home in a while," Janice said.

"Are you going to stay here?" I asked.

"You'd like that," Janice said, "wouldn't you?"

"I hate it here," I said.

"I'll make it better," Janice said.

I knew she was lying about something, hiding her true motives. Something wasn't right, that was obvious. The way she smiled and tilted her head, hopeful in her promise—we needed each other, we just didn't know how, or why, exactly.

"Where are you going to stay?" I asked.

"I'll figure something out," Janice said.

"What about your job?" I asked.

"Can we please talk about something else?" Janice asked.

Martin appeared again. He dropped a tray of chips between Janice and me.

"We didn't ask for this," Janice said.

"Complimentary," Martin said.

"We asked for margaritas," I said.

"You want to know something?" Martin asked us, as he stared through Jimi Hendrix.

"No," Janice said. "We just want to eat."

"I once lived in New Orleans," Martin said. "Before that, I lived in Missoula. Reno before that. Before that . . . who knows. I used to ride my bicycle to school. I've seen sunsets in every direction. Chances are, if you're interested in painting landscapes, I could help you out. My life is fuller than it feels. Remember that. Okay?"

Martin shuffled back outside.

"What is wrong with this place?" Janice asked.

"I don't know," I said.

"Is everyone here a freak?" Janice asked.

"I guess," I said. "Maybe."

"I don't like it here," Janice said.

"There are freaks in Chicago," I said.

"This is different," Janice said.

"There are freaks everywhere," I said.

"There are just more in Missouri," Janice said.

I shifted, rubbed my arms.

"What does that make us?" I asked.

Janice shifted, gave her hair a soft tug.

"Lost," Janice said.

"Lost," I repeated.

"Not where we belong," Janice said.

She closed her eyes, rubbed her forehead, sighed. My thumbs fidgeted on the table.

We left, went next door, got expensive frozen yogurt with too many toppings, sat on the curb thinking, and tossed our sticky containers in a garbage can when Janice came to a decision.

"I'll stay at a motel," Janice said.

"Forever?" I asked.

"You won't be here forever," Janice said.

"This isn't about me," I said.

Janice's phone kept ringing. She kept ignoring the pulsing in her pocket.

"Janice," I said, "you have to tell me."

Janice slumped into herself. A biker came close to squishing our toes.

"Let's find a place," Janice said.

THE PLACE WE found was a one-story motel off the highway, a short walk from campus, next to the Megabus stop, bordered by a strip mall and a strip club. Loka House was the kind of structure tornados flatten with ease. The front desk was vacant when we walked in. Janice slapped the bell next to a bowl of melted peppermints. She slapped it again and again and again. Sweat beads formed on her nose.

"Maybe they're closed." I tried to pull her away from the bell. She resisted and kept slapping.

"Hello!" Janice screamed.

There was a door behind the desk with five thick locks separating us from whatever lurked behind. The room in which we stood was bare, beige, and florescent. The front desk was a plywood box. If Janice kept slapping away, I thought, this entire hotel was going to implode. This wasn't a place that was built to last. Janice had sweat on her arms.

"Okay!" a voice shouted from behind the door.

"Come out here!" Janice shouted back.

"I am!" the voice answered.

"Now!" Janice shouted.

We were engaged in a strange hostage situation. One by one, the door's thick locks clicked.

"I'm coming out!" the voice said.

The fifth lock clicked and the door swung open. Out stepped a short man in tight underwear wielding a flat bat, a weapon unlike anything I've seen before. He was shirtless and potbellied, South Asian with close-cropped black hair. His emerald eyes were crazed and bloodshot.

"Is this what you want?" the man asked.

Janice and I ducked behind the front desk.

"Show yourself," the man demanded.

"We just want a room," Janice said.

"Why didn't you say so?" the man said.

"This is a hotel," Janice said, still crouched.

"A motel," the man said. "Stand up. Don't be ridiculous."

Janice and I stood up. The man was still without shirt and pants. He dropped the flat bat on the floor.

"What's your problem?" Janice asked.

"Criminals," the man said.

"We just want a room," Janice said.

I didn't know what to say, or ask for.

"Hourly?" the man asked, looking between us.

"We're not criminals," I said.

"Weekly," Janice said. "Monthly."

"*Here?*" I asked Janice. "For a *month?*"

"Maybe," Janice said. "Months."

"We have strong showerheads," the man interjected.

The front door opened behind us.

"Dad!" a voice said.

A young woman shot around the front desk, stood in front of her father, blocked his immodest presence from our eyes.

"I'm so sorry," she said before turning around to scold her topless and bottomless father in a language I didn't recognize.

"We just want a room," Janice said.

The woman pushed her father into the backroom. He didn't put up much of a fight. He did rant and rave after the door was closed and the locks were locked. The woman took deep breaths. She adjusted her ponytail and glasses. She was the tallest person in the room. She had broad shoulders that angled into a thin waist and long thin legs. She was model-like, with high cheekbones and emerald eyes—her father's eyes.

"My name's Juna," Juna said. She extended a hand in apology.

"We just need a room for a while," Janice said.

"Pardon my father," Juna said as she shuffled through a binder, looking for something.

"Is he okay?" I asked.

"Are any of us?" Juna asked.

"I'd prefer a big bed," Janice said. "And a fridge."

"Hourly?" Juna asked.

"Are there criminals around here?" I asked, stepping in, annoying Janice.

"There are criminals everywhere," Juna said.

"Your father called us criminals," I said.

"It's because we're black," Janice said to me.

"We're not racists," Juna said.

"Everyone is a little racist," Janice said.

"He's talking about the white boys," Juna said.

Juna continued to flip through her binder, half-interested in our questions.

"What white boys?" I asked.

"They think we're Arabs," Juna said.

"Huh?" I asked.

"They're idiots," Juna said.

"Will they bother us?" Janice asked.

"I don't think so," Juna said.

She found the page she was looking for. Her finger shot in the air.

"Ah!" Juna exclaimed. "We have a king-size bed with a fridge available."

"I don't know about this," I said to Janice.

"I'll take it," Janice said to Juna.

"We can keep looking," I said to Janice.

"Cash or card?" Juna said.

"Cash." Janice took the money from her pocket and slid it toward Juna. Juna took the stack without counting.

"Let me know if you need more," Janice said.

Juna nodded. She bent underneath the desk and emerged with two keys, each one dangling from an oversize chain.

"Room twenty-three," Juna said.

Janice grabbed both keys, offered me one on the way out.

Rooms at Loka House were numbered without discernable logic. The first room was 3; then 1, 6, 8, 14, 15, 18, 20, 20B, and, at the end, 23. Ten rooms, one red Jeep in the parking lot, smashed cigarette packs on the curb, windows with closed curtains facing the street; a broken ballerina statuette leaned against room 18. Room 23 had a stubborn door that needed four hard pushes before it opened. I didn't know despair had a smell.

"Are you sure about this?" I asked Janice.

She didn't answer. Instead, she moved around the room in silence, sniffing, inspecting. She peeked behind the shower curtain and whipped the closet open.

"We're safe," Janice said.

"Safe from what?" I asked.

"Sit down," Janice said.

I bounced onto the fluffy mattress. Janice sat next to me.

"Don't freak out," Janice said.

From the second I saw her sitting in my dorm room, bored and calm, I knew someone was chasing her. I knew something bad was breathing down her neck. Still, I wasn't expecting this.

Janice explained, in a voice that weakened as she went on, how everything had gone to shit.

She was working at this nightclub, she said. Her job, as she described it, was shaking her ass and getting rich people to buy expensive liquor by the overpriced bottle. These rich people would get tables in the VIP sections. Janice was responsible for getting them to show off their wealth. She got 20 percent of each bottle she sold. If the rich people who bought tables were men, and they usually were, they would pay in cash to impress Janice. Men like that, Janice thought, learned about women through music videos and movies about cool men made by loser men.

"Pathetic," she said, "throwing money around expecting me to—who knows? They're like dogs chasing cars."

One night, this bachelor party came in. Janice was assigned to their section; bachelor parties loved Janice. The bachelor party wanted Janice to dance with them, asked if she was from Chicago, asked if she still lived in South Shore. Janice told them she moved downtown first chance she got. The bachelor party couldn't believe it: this beautiful woman from their old neighborhood dancing inches away. They wanted to reminisce with her, slide into a nostalgic stream, remember the bus stops, chicken shacks, fights after school, long summer days on the beach, on the basketball courts, rushing home before dark, before the shooting started; the bachelor and his party were young and wanted to remember when they were younger. When the music stopped and the lights turned on, the bachelor party invited Janice to another bar.

Sitting in our motel room, Janice couldn't explain why she agreed to meet them.

"When you left," Janice said. "I wanted to forget South Shore. These guys seemed nice, innocent, and kind. They reminded me of you. Their faces were soft. Their suits didn't fit right. They paid in cash, said they'd wait for me at another bar, wouldn't leave until I showed up."

When Janice walked into the other bar, the bachelor party started cheering. They bought her a drink, told her to sit at their booth, asked if she wanted pizza, or fries, or chicken tenders, or a steak sandwich.

There was one guy in particular. Janice kept staring at him. He kept staring at Janice. The Best Man, a short man with glasses, a little round, cute. He picked at Janice's fries and bought her another drink. Outside, he offered Janice a cigarette, lit it with matches, blew his smoke away from her face. The Best Man told Janice about the wedding, tomorrow, back in South Shore, with all their friends and family. He said things about coming home for good. Janice asked where The Best Man lived now. He said he floated around, moved from place to place. Janice thought he was a boring salesman trying to make himself exciting.

When The Bachelor threw up in an alley, the night finished and The Best Man asked if Janice wanted to split a cab.

"Wait," I said. "Did you sleep with him?"

"I sleep with people all the time," Janice said. "Listen."

Inside Janice's apartment, The Best Man tripped over his suit pants, struggled against his tie. Under his shirt, tattoos wrapped up his arms, covered his torso, stopped at his clavicle. His body was an indecipherable inked mess. Janice kissed his neck, ear, cheeks, and lips. Before he drifted off to sleep, Janice kissed his forehead and watched the sun pushing out of Lake Michigan. She was going to wake him, kick him out, call a cab, and forgot about South Shore all over again.

"That's when I saw it," Janice said. "Across his back."

"Saw what?" I asked.

"He rolled over," Janice said.

"What did you see?" I asked.

The Best Man had REDBELTERS scrawled in block letters between his shoulder blades.

"I blinked," Janice said. "I rubbed my eyes. I thought I was dreaming. I have these nightmares all the time: I'm back in South Shore and the riot is happening again and the riot is never ending and the Redbelters are marching down the street shooting people in the chest. In these nightmares, I'm standing there watching and I can't move. I try to run. I can't. I stand there screaming. They march up to me, laughing, pointing their guns at me. I wake up sweating. When I saw that tattoo, I thought I was in a nightmare. I slapped my cheeks. I tried to breathe deep, slow."

"Janice," I said, fear tightening my lungs. "What did you do?"

She sat back down, closer to me, put her head on my shoulder.

"I touched the tattoo," Janice said. "It wasn't a dream. It was real. I touched it again, rubbed it, heard him purr."

She didn't fall back asleep. She watched the sun keep pushing up.

When The Best Man woke up, he told Janice his real name, asked if he could call her next weekend. Janice wrote his number on an old receipt. She watched him get dressed, kissed him at the door, laid back in bed, and stared at her ceiling.

"It all came back," Janice said. "These searing flashes. All the things I'd promised myself I'd do if the Redbelters came back, if I saw a Redbelter walking down the street. What they did to my life . . ."

"Janice," I said. "What did you do?"

"Remember?" Janice asked. "When we talked about choices?"

"Janice," I said.

"I told you," Janice said. "If I had a time machine."

"Janice," I said.

"I thought they were gone," Janice said.

"What did you do?" I asked.

She'd walked to her window, watched the morning traffic grind down Lake Shore Drive, tapped her head against the glass, wondered if she could leave Chicago.

She'd moved to the couch, curled up, still naked, worked through her options. She could call the police, let them know the Redbelters weren't gone, tell them about the wedding. She could call The Best Man, call him a coward and murderer, say he ruined lives, ruined her life. She could call no one. She didn't live in South Shore anymore. She didn't have to care. She could move on.

She'd opened her fridge, opened her closet, checked her drawers, and measured her life. She counted everything in her small apartment. She decided there wasn't enough to weigh her down.

She'd gone back to the window. She said goodbye to Lake Michigan. She felt her mind expand with new possibilities.

"I got dressed," Janice said. "I packed a bag. I threw up. I brushed my teeth. I took all my cash tips, this big stack I was saving to leave Chicago for good. I put that in my bag. I took a cab to the bus station. At the bus station, used a pay phone and called the cops."

"No," I said. "You didn't."

"I did," Janice said. "I told them about the wedding. I told them the Redbelters were back."

"The cops," I said. "You called the cops."

"It felt right," Janice said. "My body felt on fire and it felt right."

"The cops won't help," I said.

"They might," Janice said.

"You can't trust cops," I said.

"The Redbelters are worse," Janice said.

"They're the same," I said.

"You don't mean that," Janice said.

"They both kill people," I said.

"Not all cops kill people," Janice said.

"What if the Redbelters find out?" I said. "What if they follow you?"

"I don't care anymore," Janice said.

"Janice," I said. "They'll find you. They'll find us."

"Claude," Janice said. "This is our chance to start over. Together."

She was scared. I was scared too. I kept my eyes on the door-knob, planned the quickest exit, ignored the ringing in my ears.

I imagined Redbelters kicking the door into pieces, busting in with loaded automatic weapons. In my head, I heard rapid gunshots splashing my insides across the walls and ceiling and rug and lamps. It felt like a bad movie with cartoonish vil-lains and bumbling heroes. Heavy metal—screeching guitars, pummeled drums—rattled my brain. That screeching. All that noise. I had heard it before. Back home, standing in the street, Redbelters and cops around me—I had heard it before: impend-ing chaos howling in my face. Years ago, standing in the street, I'd decided to run home. Now, sitting in a motel room with Janice, I measured my own life. I could stay in Missouri, write my articles, play my part, translate the black experience. As I worked through my options, I saw Janice as I saw her months ago, when I decided to leave Chicago. Then, I wished I could take her with me. Now, she was here, sitting next to me, willing to start a new life together. It was just us, in a motel room, in Missouri, unsure where we would call home next.

I couldn't turn a corner and see Grandma, in the distance, protecting our porch. I couldn't run into Paul's bulging stom-ach, ask him to hold me, ask him for some wine, ask him if we were going to make it.

As I see it now, all these years later, I could've told Janice to leave. I could've walked back to my dorm room, studied for a

Sociology exam, edited my articles, gone to lunch. I could've raised my palms, backed away, shook my head—no, Janice, no, not my problem. This wasn't a movie. This was my life. I could've turned my back. Maybe I should've.

Instead, I kept my eyes on the doorknob, forgot about college, leaned forward, let the screeching come into my brain, let my heart pump and pump.

"Janice?" I said. "Why did you come here?"

"Claude," Janice said. "You know."

"Know what?" I asked.

"I need you," Janice said.

"For what?" I asked.

"I love you," Janice said.

"You do?" I asked.

"Claude," Janice said. "We can do this."

"Do what?" I asked.

"Aren't you listening?" Janice asked.

"I have to go," I said. "I can come back tonight."

"Maybe some dinner?" Janice asked. "Don't forget my bag."

She was on her back, legs straight up, perpendicular to the bed. She was stretching with her eyes closed. I imagined she was trying to relax. Deep breaths sunk her stomach and lifted her chest toward the crooked ceiling fan. There was a large spiderweb connecting all the blades. The web's maker was nowhere in sight. Janice took another breath. She was humming in a low register. Her phone vibrated, another mystery I couldn't see. Somewhere, through the walls, another phone rang, loud. There

I was, struck, surrounded by vibrations and ringing and float-ing smells and dust that felt like mist and lurking spiders capa-ble of sewing complex webs.

"Maybe tacos," Janice said from her back, legs still upright, eyes shut.

"Maybe," I said.

"Come on," Janice said.

I wrapped my arms around her legs, looked over her feet, held her legs tighter, looked into her closed eyes.

Her eyes opened, met mine. In that quick moment, we hur-tled through time and found ourselves in my bedroom, back home, years ago, feeling each other for the first time, fumbling in our young love. Now, I held her legs tighter. Her soft stare didn't break.

"I love you too," I said.

"I know," Janice said, smiled, blew me a kiss.

"I won't take too long," I said.

"Claude," Janice said. "Watch out."

"Watch out for what?" I asked.

"In my bag," Janice said.

"What?" I asked, paused next to the door.

"There's a gun," Janice said.

"Janice," I said, slumped.

"For protection," Janice said.

"Janice," I said, slumped further down.

"Protect yourself," Janice said.

"Where did you get a gun?" I asked.

"We're from Chicago," Janice said. "I need to feel safe."

I heard her lock the door behind me, wiggle the doorknob to make sure. When I stepped outside, my first instinct was to check the parking lot for suspicious characters. The only person out there leaned against the red Jeep. On first glance, he was dressed too nicely for this setting—dress shirt, khakis, sunglasses with some gold in the frame, flickering. He looked up from a small book, slid his glasses down his nose.

"Yo," he said to me.

"Yo," I said back.

"Want some pussy?" he asked.

"Naw," I said.

"Want some blow?" he asked.

"Naw," I said.

He slid his glasses back over his eyes, went back to reading his book and flickering in the afternoon sun.

I had to get Janice out of here. We couldn't make a life in this parking lot. Our children needed space to grow and play. We needed a place with untouched land stretched over painted hills, bordered by rivers and cut with streams. A place to hide and cool down, that's what we needed. I turned and watched our door, waited for Janice to appear and tell me to stay, tell me she had a plan and that plan involved leaving right now, at this second. I stood like that until a passing fire truck shook me awake. I was late. I had to get to the journalism office.

The Prairie Executioner #2

SIMONE WAS SITTING across from Whitney when I walked in, the Pit like a solid lake between them. I sat next to Simone.

"You're late," Whitney said to me. I wasn't.

"I'm sorry," I said.

"Like I was saying," Whitney said, with her eyes on me.

"You were saying," Simone said to Whitney, "that you want us to speak for all black people."

"You could say that," Whitney said. "I wouldn't say that."

"What would you say?" Simone asked. She crossed her arms and tilted her chair back, almost fell back on the scuffed floor, caught herself.

"I'd say," Whiney said, "that both of you are expected to investigate important issues."

"So," Simone said, "you want us to be grateful?"

"Yes," Whitney said.

I put my hand on Simone's shoulder. I wanted to stop her from murdering Whitney. Simone slapped me away. After she slapped my hand, Simone slapped both her hands on the Pit. Whitney and I winced—that rocklike wood must have hurt. Simone, though, didn't show it. She kept her face straight. She looked at Whitney's heart. Whitney slid back, further scuffed the scuffed floor.

"I didn't mean—" Whitney tried to say.

"I'll do it," Simone said. "I just want you to know how fucked up it is."

Somewhere above our heads, someone dropped something light. We heard it bounce through our silence. We kept our eyes on Simone. Simone's eyes, however, were sliding through Whitney's body, moving now from her heart to her soul. Whitney was scared. And I wasn't sure why. It didn't seem, to me, that Whitney thought Simone capable of spontaneous murder. No, Whitney wasn't scared; she was terrified. Scared people can summon a response to their fear. Terror freezes a person in their seat, makes their brown hair turn white. Whitney was terrified of what most terrifies white people in liberal-minded professional environments—Whitney didn't want Simone to call her a racist. Whitney was terrified of being labeled. I would've felt sorry for her, tried to calm the situation; I would've tried to see the tension-filled scene from her perspective; I would've tried to imagine Whitney as a high school junior arguing with her father about the proper term to call black people—*African American*, not *nigger*; I would've imagined her last fall, out on the Missouri highway with a busload of other Obama volunteers, canvassing for hope and change and a new world, one different from the world that raised them; I would've imagined her reading James Baldwin in a café, shaking her head and furrowing her brow at injustice—I would've helped her out, if Simone wasn't right. But Simone was right: this *was* fucked up. I wanted to hear Simone call Whitney a racist. I wanted to see Whitney's brown hair turn white.

Simone didn't call her a racist. Instead, Simone took out her notebook and poised her pen over paper. Whitney emerged from her terror spell, shaken and intact. This was Simone's meeting now.

"So," Simone began, "did you know there are fourteen statues of Thomas Jefferson on campus?"

"No," Whitney said.

"Did you know," Simone continued, "that Thomas Jefferson was a rapist and a racist?"

"No," Whitney said, shaking her head and furrowing her brow at injustice.

"Do we, as a campus," Simone went on, "need fourteen different monuments to violent patriarchy and racism?"

"No," Whitney said. "No, no, no, no, no."

She would've said no forever if Simone hadn't jumped in.

"My history professor," Simone said, "thinks we should remove all the statues."

"All of them?" Whitney asked.

Simone's eyes went back into Whitney's soul.

"All of them," Simone said.

"Okay," Whitney said. "Sounds promising."

Simone, satisfied for a brief moment, relaxed into her chair. They both looked at me.

"What are you thinking?" Simone asked me.

"I don't care too much about Thomas Jefferson," I said.

"Well," Simone said, "you should."

Whitney, sensing another quake coming, stepped in to save me.

"I mean," Whitney said, with her chin in her chest, "do you have any story ideas?"

"Nothing interesting," I said.

"Nothing?" Whitney asked.

"Nothing?" Simone asked.

"You don't care about anything?" Whitney asked.

I imagined Janice in the motel bed, still in her stiff pose, legs toward the ceiling, unable to move. The sun had set—did she have the energy to turn on the lights? Was she safe? I thought of the danger that had her surrounded. I had to get back.

"I'll think of something tonight," I said.

"Claude," Whitney said. "Do you work here?"

"Don't you care about anything?" Simone asked.

"I don't know," I said. I stood up to leave, was ready to run. Connie Stove appeared in the doorway.

"What was that I heard?" Connie Stove asked. "Did I hear hesitation?"

"I just have to go," I said.

"Sit down," Connie Stove said.

I sat down. Simone and Whitney shifted in their chairs. I hoped Simone would come to my defense, stop what was coming. She didn't. She lowered her eyes and picked at her fingernails. I was alone. Connie Stove glided toward us.

"What is the hesitation?" Connie Stove asked.

I tried to respond. She raised both her pointer fingers, closed her eyes. I mumbled about needing to leave. I disturbed her rhythm. She started over.

"What is the hesitation?" Connie Stove repeated. "Don't you feel the moment's urgency? Does the ground not feel fragile under your step? Acres, I say. Acres of progress unwind before us. We are living in a new age. When I was eighteen and taking acid tabs like cough drops—on fire, the world was on fire. I would sit in my dorm room with Lucinda, stare at our radio, construct maps of the patriarchy, and plot ways to turn the establishment into embers. Lucinda and I—dear Lucinda— could stare at that radio for hours. And do you know why? Put your hand down. I'll tell you why. We were listening to images of horror and the horror never stopped. Vietnam, Mississippi, Chicago, 1600 Pennsylvania Avenue—all of it was burning down and we couldn't look away. And where was the epicenter? The eye of the hurricane—where was that? Where was the earth cracking in two, three, four? Where did the storm troopers run up against immovable blockades? Put your hand down. I'll tell you where: college campuses. Did you hear me? I'll say it again: college campuses. Lucinda and I watched our dorm walls melt into psychedelic streams; we watched the black students take over the bursar's office; we watched professors join our comrades in the struggle; we looked Nixon's storm troopers in their terrified eyes. We looked at our radio and saw images of young men coming back from the jungle in acres of boxes. The bodies kept flowing. Lucinda and I dreamed of those boxes and those boys. We were angry. When our dreams turned to nightmares, we would wake up screaming. We stopped going to class. We ordered pizza. We didn't take the pizza boxes out to the trash. Acid turned our minds into glorious sponges. We turned the pizza boxes into dioramas of public monuments. We made a pizza-box Lincoln Memorial and stomped on it until the greased cardboard turned to mush. We threw a pizza-box White House out our window and cheered as it got caught in a draft and flew out of town. We were heroes, Lucinda and I. Every student was a hero, passionate, driven, moral, tripping off life and potent chemicals. That's how it was back then. And we won. Damn it. We got what we asked for. We got women's studies and black studies and Latino studies and professors of all colors. We got the diversity we wanted. So what do you want? So what are you going to do? Put your hand down. I'll tell you . . ."

My mind wandered back to Janice. The initial shock of seeing her had started to wear off. I wasn't confused anymore, dumbfounded. I was happy she was so close. I had forgotten the ease I felt around her. Even if she was in desperate trouble and I didn't know how to help, I knew that we would figure out a way. We always did. I had to get back to her. Did she want me to stay in the motel with her, in the same bed? Should I bring my shampoo and body wash back with me? What should we do with that bag? What was I going to tell Kenneth? Who cared what Kenneth thought? How long could Janice and I stay safe?

What did we need to figure out? Why couldn't we run away tonight? The gun. I remembered the gun and tightened.

Simone punched me in the ribs.

"What?" I asked, angry for my disturbed thoughts.

Simone tilted her head toward Connie Stove. Connie Stove's arms were outstretched toward me, pleading.

"Yeah?" I asked.

"I'll ask again," Connie Stove said. "You, Claude, what do you want out of this world?"

I thought of Janice tucked under her motel covers, smiling in her sleep. I thought of myself next to her, awake, thinking of the ways I could make her happy.

I couldn't tell Connie Stove that.

"I have to think about it," I said.

"Well," Connie Stove said, deflated, "think hard. And fast. Time doesn't slow down for slow movers."

"Okay," I said. "I have to go."

"Dismissed," Connie Stove said.

Simone caught up to me on the stairwell. She grabbed my arm to slow me. Our differing momentums almost took us down.

"What the fuck was that?" Simone asked my back. I hadn't turned around.

"I have to go," I said.

"What's your problem?" Simone asked, after jumping in front of me, blocking my way forward.

"Please," I said.

"No," Simone said. "That was fucked up."

I blew past her; she followed at my heels, up the stairs, out the door, over fallen leaves, and across campus.

"Don't you care?" Simone asked. "Don't you care about anything?"

"Now is not a good time," I said.

"Sure," Simone said. "This project is fucked up. All these white people taking advantage of our blackness."

We almost collided with a skateboarder.

"Sure," Simone continued. "Whitney and Connie are crazy, in different ways, for different reasons. I hate it when people define me by my race."

Simone kept up with me. I was jogging and didn't realize until I hurdled a person, hunched over, picking up fallen papers, spilled backpack contents. Simone hurdled also.

"Sure," Simone continued. "I hate it when people don't care about my knowledge of South Asian history or pre–World War I politics. I'm a well-rounded person. I'm not just an expert on blackness. I don't think I'm an expert on blackness. How can any one person be an expert on blackness? It's not like there's only one kind of blackness. There are differing levels of exposure, differences in environment, different people. Watch out!"

A car ran a stop sign. Simone stuck her arm across my chest, saved my life. I didn't thank her. I kept jogging. She kept jogging.

"Sure," Simone continued. "I'm not interested in journalism as a profession. I'd make a better lawyer, I hear. I've heard I'm too smart to make a career in journalism. You need a narrow focus to chase down leads and crack stories and survive on a beat. Or you need a broad, shallow focus to appeal to different

readers from different walks of life. Like a syndicated colum-
nist. You know?"

We both stopped in front of my dorm, faced each other,
unsure how to finish, unsure how we got there. I'd thought
Simone was angry with me. Looking at her face, underneath
a streetlamp's burgeoning orange glow, in the fresh dark—she
was worried.

"Tell me," Simone said. "Are you okay?"

"I don't know," I said. "Now's not a good time."

"Sure," Simone said. "Maybe later."

She looked at her watch, tried to decide how much time I
deserved.

"Fuck," Simone said. "I'm late for Biology."

I wasn't expecting her to hug me like that: big and deep.
She shoved her head into my chest and left it there for a couple heartbeats; her hands shook against my back. She let go,
sprinted away. I considered sprinting after her, catching up,
walking her to biology, telling her she was right, of course she
was right. I saw myself saying I wanted to talk more. I saw the
two of us at graduation, laughing about freshman year. I saw
us moving to Kansas City, working at *The Star*, filing stories
about county fairs and junior proms, driving home together,
kissing each other goodnight, waking up in our studio apartment, laughing over coffee and eggs. I saw us happy and realis-
tic, pragmatic and normal. I saw us working through my past
traumas. I saw her jaw-dropping when I told her about Janice,
Chicago, the day Janice showed up in Missouri. I saw her appre-
ciating my rational decisions.

I watched her disappear behind a bus.

Janice punched back into my mind.

I slid into the elevator at the dorm as it closed. A man and a dozen large plastic water jugs were waiting for me. The man apologized—he had to hit every floor, drop off two jugs, until he reached the top.

"Every month," he said, "unless there's an emergency."

"People need free drinking water," the man said. He spoke with conviction.

He started talking about his life, all the turns that brought him into an elevator with jugs of water. He started with his childhood in East Texas. I heard Simone's voice still echoing around my brain.

What did I care about?

I thought of the first time I saw Janice, in her pigtails, sitting with me at the back of the auditorium.

I thought of Paul and Grandma explaining my future at the dinner table. I never felt my destiny like they did. I didn't sense greatness lurking. I had come to understand my average place in the world. Simone—she was someone capable of rising into the stratosphere. I could see it then, in the elevator, paused at the fourth floor as the man lugged two jugs into the hallway—Simone was going to change the world. What was I going to do?

First, I had to get back to Janice.

The man told me about his first wife, or his second wife, or maybe a wife he only dreamed about. I wasn't paying attention. I jumped out of the elevator a few floors beneath mine, sprinted up the stairs to my room, out of breath.

KENNETH WAS STANDING over a large American flag, the kind you see fluttering outside town halls and large museums.

"Good," Kenneth said. "You can help me."

"What is this?" I asked, as I walked across the wide stripes.

The flag extended from wall to wall. It covered both our beds and desks. Dead bugs made brown and green streaks across the frayed fabric.

I liked it there: decorated with filth, awkward, squeezed, wrinkled, improper. Here, I could walk across it and feel powerful. It was cloth. Cloth and ripped stiches. I walked in a small circle over the lower stripes, jogged in place, walked to the stars, bent down, flicked some. The flag was something I didn't think about. When I saw it flying proud atop tall metal poles, it didn't seem meant for me. It was always far away. Nobody flew flags in South Shore. Here, now, I could walk on it. It felt tangible, not a big deal.

"I found it," Kenneth said. "I need help folding it."

I lifted the flag off my bed. Janice's duffel bag hadn't been moved. I picked it up and walked back to the door. I took a heavy step and extended a small rip on the lower stripes.

"Watch it!" Kenneth yelled.

He rushed to the rip, dropped to his knees, and investigated.

I went into my closet, grabbed a few shirts, some underwear, socks, and pair of jeans. I tossed the armload of clothes into Janice's duffel bag. I couldn't get it closed on the first few tries.

"Where are you going?" Kenneth asked.

"I'm moving out," I said.

"Who's going to help me?" Kenneth, now standing upright, gestured at the ripped and strained flag underneath our feet. He was close to tears. I didn't have time to console him. I didn't think Kenneth was a bad person. I thought, maybe, that he wasn't born in the right universe. He belonged in a world without time and emergencies. Kenneth's proper world, I thought, was made of beanbag mountains and lava-lamp rivers.

I put a hand on his shoulder.

"Another day," I said.

"Yes," Kenneth said. "Another day. Yes."

Kenneth was smiling at limitless space when I left him.

The man with the jugs was in the elevator again, jugless, exhausted. He leaned against the elevator's back wall. I kept right in front of the door, so close that the motion sensors wouldn't let the doors close. I took a step back, dropped my bag.

"You're in a rush," the man said.

"Yes," I said.

"Love?" the man asked.

"I think so," I said.

I kept my back to him.

"I'd do anything for my cats," the man said. "Humans and me never worked out. Opening a can of tuna for my cats—that's what makes me happy."

The elevator opened and a couple stepped in, holding hands, whispering and giggling. I heard the man sigh behind me.

I ran toward Janice, careful with her bag.

Tacos and Hendrix

I WAS HALFWAY across campus when Janice called me.

"Bring tacos," she said.

She wanted Martin's. Maybe, she said, he was just having a bad afternoon. She wanted everything on the menu. She was starving. Hurry, she said. Famished, she said.

"Okay," I said.

"Not just tacos," Janice said. "Enchiladas too. Let's feast. Use my money."

I headed toward Martin's. The duffel bag swung against my leg. I kept telling myself to act casual, cool, don't sweat. I couldn't stop sweating. The bag was heavier than expected. That didn't help the sweating. I didn't want to go back to Martin's. I wanted to get back to Janice. In that moment, I think, I learned something about love and devotion. If she wanted tacos and enchiladas, I was going to get her tacos and enchiladas and every type of salsa. Still, I would do it for Janice.

First, I had to look in the bag. I had to see. I had to hold the gun.

Martin's was empty when I walked in. Martin was standing in the kitchen, staring at a wall behind the stove. He was following something with his eyes. I couldn't tell what. I hit a bell on the counter. I hit it again and again and again. Martin finally acknowledged the sound.

"What's that?" Martin asked the wall.

"I need some food," I said.

"I can make that happen," Martin said.

"Can I get one of everything?" I asked.

Martin moved his eyes to the stovetop.

"I can make that happen," Martin said.

"Can I use your bathroom?" I asked.

"In this world," Martin said, "we try to replicate Utopia."

I found the bathroom to my right. I locked the door and, just in case, held the doorknob with one hand. With my free hand, I hoisted the duffel bag onto the sink, unzipped it, moved the clothes around, felt for hard metal, and found it, black like most guns I saw on T.V., a handgun. I gripped it. I looked at the barrel, saw numbers and letters, saw 9 mm. I wondered, if it came down to it, if I could pull the trigger in time. I wondered if I could save us.

The bathroom spun; neon stickers and newspaper clippings about Woodstock twirled in a delirious hurricane. Richard

Nixon's face hung in the urinal. I puked a clear and nervous liquid on his bulbous nose.

Martin wasn't cooking when I crept out of the bathroom. He stared into an open cooler.

"Excuse me," I said.

He didn't twitch.

"Hey," I said again. "Yo!" I yelled.

Startled, Martin looked up.

"No need for that," Martin said.

"I'm in a hurry," I said.

"The world isn't going to spin faster," Martin said.

"Listen," I said. "My girlfriend is starving. She wants your fucking tacos. And your fucking enchiladas. I am in a hurry."

"I can't rush the process," Martin said.

"Are you insane!?" I yelled.

The door opened behind me.

"Everything alright in here?" a voice asked.

I turned around and saw a cop, hands on her waist. The duffel bag fell out of my hands with a thud.

Martin pointed a crooked finger at me.

"This righteous-brother fascist is rushing my process," Martin said.

"I don't know what that means," the cop said. She moved next to the duffel bag. She stared at the sweat on my forehead and nose.

"I just want food," I said, "and he won't make it."

"This is art," Martin said. "I'm not some machine."

"Martin," the cop said. "We've talked about this."

Martin turned sheepish.

"It's not fair," Martin said.

"The customers come first," the cop said.

"Da Vinci didn't think of his customers," Martin protested.

"Yes, he did," the cop said.

Martin grumbled and went about arranging pots and pans over open flames. He removed slabs of chicken, beef, and pork from the cooler.

"What did you order?" the cop asked me while looking at Martin work. He was good, maybe an artist.

"My girlfriend is hungry," I said.

"Hey, Martin," the cop said, "I'll have what he's having."

Martin grunted into a sizzling pan. The three of us listened to hot and popping oil. The cop drummed her fingers on the counter. She nodded to her off-tempo beat. I kept my eyes on her belt—pepper spray, gun, and handcuffs. I wondered which she would use first if I obeyed my gut and made a run for it. Quick mental math convinced me otherwise: distance from the door plus weight of the bag plus my suspicious appearance equaled no escape. I heard Paul's voice over Martin's cooking: "Never run from cops; they'll kill your ass."

"Just arrive?" the cop asked me while looking at the duffel bag.

"Huh?" I asked.

"New in town?" The cop tried again.

"I'm a student," I said. "My girlfriend's hungry."

"Good for you," the cop said. "It's nice to meet someone so early on."

"We knew each other in Chicago," I said. "She's like my sister."

The cop noticed something about me, something that made her eyes go slant, made her brow furrow. I wiped the sweat from my forehead.

"Chicago?" the cop asked. "What the hell are you doing here?"

"I write for the paper," I said. "I want to be a journalist."

When I said it out loud—journalist—it felt false. But that falseness felt good, freeing. If I didn't want to be a journalist, what did I want?

"Cops are like journalists," the cop interrupted. "Most people can't stand them."

"I love cops," I blurted.

She narrowed her eyes. I couldn't see her eyeballs through her squinting. Or my brain was shrinking out of fear, not working like it should. She nudged the duffel bag with her shoe.

"What you got in there?" the cop asked.

"Clothes," I blurted. I tried to control my blurting and sweating and shaking.

"Feels like bricks," the cop said.

I kept my eyes on her belt.

"Shoes." I tried not to blurt. I didn't want to faint. I held onto the counter. It was sticky and warm. I tried my math again—could I make it out before she gunned me down? Would I have to get the gun out and fire back? Could I make it to Janice, have a chance to express my love, before I bled out?

"This is your girlfriend's bag," the cop said, "isn't it?"

Would I end up in prison for a gun that wasn't mine? Would they go easy on me if I confessed? I could take the blame. I'd go down for Janice. I'd write her letters from my cell. Some prison gang would take me in, show me the ropes, keep the white supremacists away, help me in the weight room. Paul and Grandma would visit me. Janice would send me photos of herself in a bathrobe, lounging on a long chair next to a pool. Tasteful lingerie pictures would cover my prison-cell walls.

The cop kicked my duffel bag again.

"Books?" she asked.

"Shoes," I said, again, with force.

"It doesn't feel like shoes." The cop placed her hands on her belt. One hand next to the gun; one set of fingertips on the pepper spray.

"They're shoes," I said. Sweat ran down my legs, into my socks.

"Can I see?" the cop asked. "I bet they're cool-looking shoes. Fashion stuff."

"She's protective," I said.

"She won't mind," the cop said.

Deceit is a skill, I learned. And it was a skill I didn't have. Somewhere in the criminal world, there existed an expert that could direct an inquisitive cop away from a mysterious bag. I was no expert criminal. I was, without a doubt, fucked and scared shitless.

"I can't," I said.

"Sure you can," the cop said.

"I won't," I said.

"Why not?" the cop asked.

"My girlfriend's hungry," I said. "I have to get back."

"She won't mind," the cop said.

The cop leaned down to unzip the duffel bag. I was going to scream about my rights as an American citizen. If that failed, I was going to kick the cop in the ribs and bust out of there. Before I had the chance to do anything, however, Martin emitted a coyote-like shriek, a haunting laugh. The cop jolted up. Martin was at the counter, holding two large paper bags in his arms.

"I am a genius," Martin said. "Enjoy my work."

I took my paper bag; the cop didn't take hers. She turned back to me, back to the duffel bag, back to me, back to the duffel bag.

Her mouth started to open.

Her knees started to bend toward the duffel bag.

Her hands reached down.

Her radio went off—some code I didn't understand followed by a description of a suspect. Intoxicated and unwieldy, I heard.

"Not again," the cop said. She snatched her paper bag from Martin, took off without glancing back at me. A gust twirled into me when she slammed the door. I collapsed onto the duffel bag. I was careful not to spill the food. Martin peeked over the counter, down at me.

"Time for a smoke," Martin said. "Sixty dollars."

JANICE WASN'T IN bed when I walked in. I called out for her. She called back from the bathroom. She told me to come in.

Her body was sunk in a bath, covered with bubbles. Her head rested on a folded towel; a washcloth rested on her eyes. I could only see her mouth, smiling. I sat on the toilet and had all my thoughts confirmed: I wanted to devote my life to running her errands. I dropped the duffel bag on the crusted tiles. Janice, startled by the thud, lifted up the washcloth.

"How did it go?" she asked.

"Fine," I said. "Are you still hungry?"

"You are my fucking hero," Janice said.

She stood up and flicked bubbles off her naked body. I turned my head away. She put a wet hand on my shoulder. She put another hand on my head, twisted me toward her. Our faces were close. Small drops dripped from her eyelashes onto my cheeks. I leaned in. She hugged me into her naked stomach. I wrapped my arms around her waist. Her smooth and wet flesh against my cheek—I don't know. It made me cry. I didn't break down. Just, something about her skin against mine, something about the steam around us.

Something about our desperate situation, fear, pressing down on us. In that moment, it was too much. I didn't want to let go. Still, we had to leave soon. We couldn't stay in that bathroom forever. We had to eat, leave Missouri. At some point, we'd stop running; at some point, we'd stop treading unsettled water and move toward shore. I didn't want to let her go.

She held me closer. I put my chin in her belly button. My red eyes met her red eyes. Her tears fell on my face. She rubbed my head, patted my shoulders, held my cheeks in her hands, wiped my eyes, wiped my nose. I kept my arms around her waist.

"What are we going to do?" Janice asked.

"We're going to make it," I said.

I meant it.

"I'm scared," Janice said. "I'm hungry."

"Me too," I said. "Let's eat."

While she dried off, I unrolled a towel on the bed. One by one, I removed hot tinfoil balls from the paper bag. I arranged the salsas in a neat row—shades of green, red, orange, and champagne yellow. Tacos, burritos, enchiladas, and quesadillas, squished and imperfect, filled the room with hot spices.

Janice emerged from the bathroom wrapped in a towel.

We sat before our feast.

"I forgot," Janice said. "Hold up."

Janice bounced up, disturbed our dinner, and ran back into the bathroom. She emerged, for a second time, with a thin joint between her thumb and pointer.

"This will help," Janice said. She pulled a lighter from her towel's folds.

"Can we smoke in here?" I asked.

"From what I can tell," Janice said, "we can do anything in here."

"Where did you get that?" I asked.

"Some guy in the parking lot," Janice said. "He said it's from the Mongolian Steppe."

"Is that good?" I asked.

Janice stood up on the bed, removed the smoke alarm's batteries, lit the joint, remained standing, twisted her hips, blew smoke from her nose, blew me a sharp kiss, winked in my direction, closed her eyes, sat down, took my hand, placed the joint between my pointer and thumb.

"Let's find something crazy to watch," Janice said.

She was in denial, pretending. She kept smiling, laughing at nothing, touching my arms, legs, shoulders, and head. I smiled back, laughed with her, sank into her denial, enjoyed myself.

We ripped into the hot tinfoil balls. Smoke settled around our heads. There was a documentary about ancient Egypt on a fuzzy station. The gist, I think, was that black pharaohs don't get enough credit. Janice booed at the British narrator.

"Tell me something I don't know," Janice said over and over.

She snatched up the remote. Beans and lettuce spilled out of her shrimp burrito.

We settled for a moment on women's college volleyball.

"If I had a body like that," Janice said, "I'd kill every man with my bare hands."

"What about me?" I asked.

Janice took a series of violent bites. She poured salsa into her burrito and considered my position in her alternate reality. I suckled on a barbeque chicken taco.

"I'd kill you last," Janice decided. She broke into a suffocating laugh. I slapped her back to keep her from choking. She regained her composure, kept flipping channels.

We landed on a show about inept criminals. A beige sedan sped down a California highway, or was it Texas? Wherever it was, the highway was wide and sun-splashed. We watched from a helicopter's point of view. Close behind the speeding beige sedan, a herd of cop cars blared and swerved. A gravel-voiced narrator told us the beige sedan was filled with stolen cash. The beige sedan collided with a pickup truck and kept going. The cops followed the beige sedan off the expressway into a tree-lined neighborhood. The neighborhood, from above, reminded me of home. Janice and I watched as the driver crashed into a telephone pole and was surrounded, within seconds, by angry cops with their guns pulled. Janice changed the station. Her breaths were hard. Her eyes bulged.

"Holy shit," Janice said. "That's us."

I took stock of our situation: smoke around our heads, destroyed takeout on our bed, cars speeding down a nearby highway, distant moaning through the walls. Except, I didn't think our story would end with a chase and a crash and aerial footage.

"We'll get out of this," I said.

"How?" Janice asked.

I didn't know.

"We'll find a way," I said.

"I hope so," Janice said. "Otherwise, we're dead."

She put her burrito on the towel and the salsa-soaked contents spilled out. She turned away from me, curled into a ball, sighed, and pretended to sleep.

Sociology #2

I FAKE-SLEPT NEXT to Janice for hours, stared at the digital clock on the nightstand, thought about our options. Running wasn't our only choice. We could call the cops, ask them to protect us, hope Missouri cops would be different from Chicago cops. During the riot, the last time I had asked the cops for protection, they'd pushed me away. I heard their bullhorns shaking my brain; I saw their riot shields aligned and impenetrable.

Eleven turned into midnight.

I turned over and faced Janice's back. I drew tiny animals on her shoulder with my fingertip: a giraffe over a crocodile over a flamingo over an elephant over a hawk or falcon or eagle or vulture. I pressed my palm against her shoulder. Her breaths were deep and slow. I kept my hand there and closed my eyes, tried to fall into her rhythm. I moved closer, put my arm around her stomach, my chin on her neck. I wanted to whisper something soothing into her dreams. I pushed my legs against hers. I wanted to feel like one person.

Her stomach moved, an intense bubbling. Stress, I thought. Fear, probably.

"It's okay," I whispered into her neck.

I felt her jaw move. Her stomach kept turning.

"I'm here," I said. "It's okay."

I held her closer.

"Janice," I said. "I love you."

First, the bubbling in her stomach traveled up her throat and escaped in a stream of pungent gas. I put a hand over my nose. Then, in a second wave, the bubbling vibrated against my crotch. I rolled away, dug my face into a pillow. The pillow didn't help. I decided to get some fresh air, something to drink. With disdain, I looked at the ravaged fare in our trash can, a disheveled mixture of beans, meat, cheese, and tortillas.

I kissed Janice on the cheek, found cash in her wallet, and locked the door behind me.

The parking lot was full and alive. Couples moved between motel rooms and backseats, smoking cigarettes, laughing in hushed tones. Most of the men were old and worn down. Their companions wore dresses and heels too unstable for the uneven pavement. Everyone was having a separate party. There was no greater sense of community. I stood in front of our door and watched until an old man with tropical birds on his shirt told me to stop staring at his lady, who was bored and strong enough to toss him into their room. The tall streetlamps over the parking lot flickered over the haunting scene.

I approached a tall woman cradling a sleeping short man on the curb.

"Excuse me," I said. "What are cops like down here?"

"I'm not doing anything illegal," the tall woman whispered.

"That's not what I meant," I said.

"If you call the cops," the tall woman whispered, "they'll come and shoot you."

"How do you know?" I asked.

"You're black," the tall woman whispered. "They're cops."

"I won't call the cops," I said.

The tall woman shushed me and pointed to the short man, shifting in his dreams.

"Sorry," I said. "I'm so sorry."

"He's a soft heart," the tall woman said. "He's a big dreamer."

"Sorry," I said again.

I headed to the main office.

Juna and her father were sitting in foldout chairs in front of a small TV with long cracks forming an X on the screen. They had a bucket of popcorn between them, big sodas in their laps.

"Excuse me," I said.

"Hourly?" Juna asked, without turning around.

"I already have a room," I said.

"No refunds," the father said.

"I'm looking for a gas station," I said, "or something open late."

Something happened on the screen that made Juna jump out of her chair and clap in a short and furious burst. She turned around and noticed me.

"You need something?" Juna asked.

"Just a place that's open late," I repeated. "A place to buy some stuff."

"All the liquor stores are closed," the father said.

"You can get a drink at the strip club," Juna said.

"Not like that," I said. I craned my head around Juna, tried to make out the moving images in front of her.

"What are you watching?" I asked.

"Cricket," the father said.

"What's that?" I asked.

"Are you serious?" Juna asked me.

"Americans only watch football," the father said to his daughter. "Americans only like violence."

"I only watch basketball," I said.

"That's because you've never seen cricket," Juna said.

"What is it?" I asked.

"If I explained it," the father said, "you wouldn't understand."

"You want to watch?" Juna asked.

Somewhere outside, a car alarm exploded in the night. The father jumped up, ran outside, shouted loud threats about respecting other people and maintaining civility. He came back inside and sat down.

"What did I miss?" the father asked.

"Sure," I said. "I'll watch for a little bit."

Juna went into the backroom and came back with a stool for me. I took a seat between them. I didn't know what I was watching. There were two people with bats and helmets. One person, on another team it seemed, ran and threw a ball at one of the batters, who hit the ball. The two batters switched places. The camera showed a cheering crowd going mad, jumping up and waving flags.

"What just happened?" I asked.

"If I explained it," the father said, "you wouldn't understand."

"India against England," Juna said. "You wouldn't understand."

"You're from India?" I asked.

"I'm from St. Louis," Juna said.

"No you're not," the father said. "You're from Mumbai."

"I've never been to Mumbai," Juna said.

The father rolled his eyes at her, put his hand on my shoulder.

"Where are you from?" the father asked me.

"Chicago," I said.

"No," the father said. "You're from Africa."

"Dad!" Juna reached across me and punched her father in the shoulder, hard and with genuine intent to hurt.

"What?" the father asked. "It's true."

"I've never been to Africa," I said.

"We are Indian," the father said. "And you are African."

"I'm sorry," Juna said to me. "He's old."

"Old has nothing to do with it," the father said. "I am proud. You are not."

"I don't want to go back," I said.

"I hear Africa is beautiful," the father said.

"I can't believe this." Juna had her head between her legs.

"Not Africa," I said. "Chicago. I don't want to go back to Chicago."

"You want to stay here?" Juna asked, with disbelief. A car alarm rattled outside We didn't move. The noise continued at a disturbing rhythm. It was unlike any car alarm I had heard—frail, desperate, hopeless, hanging in there. After a few gasping cycles, someone put it down.

"Not here," I said.

"What's wrong with here?" the father asked.

"Some nights," Juna said, "I am convinced this is hell on earth."

"This is our family," the father said, wounded.

"Our rooms are filled with illicit sex," Juna said. "Our parking lot is a freak show."

"I'm not having illicit sex," I said.

Juna and her father sucked their teeth, shook their heads, rolled their eyes, just about fell out of their chairs; the father choked on popcorn and soda; Juna couldn't look me in the eyes.

"Anyway," Juna said, "this isn't paradise."

"Where do you want to go?" I asked.

"How about Chicago?" Juna asked herself.

"What about India?" the father asked. "Or Africa? Why not Mars?"

"You're angry," Juna said.

"I'm disappointed," the father said.

"If you keep getting angry," Juna said, "your heart will dissolve."

"That doesn't make sense," the father said.

"You know what I mean," Juna said.

"This place is my life," the father said. He was standing now, waving his hands in all directions. I was standing too, except I was by the door, waiting to escape.

"We could make a new life," Juna said.

"You sound like your mother," the father said.

"Is that a bad thing?" Juna asked.

Something happened on the TV and they both gasped. Then they cheered. The father leaped to his feet; Juna remained in her chair, arms stretched upward, fingers wiggling.

"No," the father said. "It's not a bad thing."

A new scene unfolded. Father and daughter were back on the same page: consumed by a game I didn't understand. They looked back at me, ashamed, I think, a little, for letting a stranger eavesdrop on their familial secrets. I wanted to tell them that I didn't care, that I appreciated their honesty. I needed honesty in big refreshing quantities. I wanted to thank them.

I didn't have the chance.

"Those assholes," the father said. He was up and in the backroom before I could turn around.

"You should go," Juna said. She crouched behind the desk. She screamed something in Hindi, I think, back at her father. He screamed something back. She nodded.

I didn't have the chance.

White Boys

//

THEY CAME AS a stumbling human chain, eyes glazed. Six of them filed through the door as I tried to exit. They wore matching red shirts with handsome bald eagle portraits printed on the front. Across their backs, in big yellow letters: DON'T TREAD ON ME. I moved behind the front desk and stood next to Juna. She gave me an apologetic glance. Once they were assembled in front of us, whiskey and cigarette smoke leaking from their mouths and pores, someone asked for a room.

"We need a place to party!"

"I need to break something!"

"I feel alive!"

"I'm sorry," Juna told them. "We don't have any rooms available."

"We are good Americans!"

"We are true Americans!"

"We deserve a true American homestead for the night!"

"We need a home base!"

"I apologize," Juna said. "We don't have any rooms available."

"Do you work for Obama?"

"Are you anti-freedom?"

"Is this the Middle East?"

"Are we at war with you?"

"Is this a desert shithole?"

"You do work for Obama!"

"I work for myself," Juna said. "And we don't have any rooms available."

Unable to break Juna's resolve, they turned their drunken attention on me.

"Brother," a bearded one said to me, "can't you help us party?"

He was pathetic. He was sad, on the verge of tears. If he didn't party soon—what was he going to do? He was lost and scared, empty, hopeless. I imagined him in a library, or any quiet setting; I imagined him struggling with his own thoughts.

I stammered as the white boys focused on me. I put my hands up and moved closer to Juna. Our hips touched. We shook against each other.

"You look like Obama."

"You are a secret agent."

"You are what's wrong with this country!"

Their white faces turned red. Sweat slid from their foreheads. Their stench intensified.

"I can't take this anymore!"

"This is our country!"

"We want it back!"

"We will take it back!"

They started to come around the front desk.

Behind us, the door slammed.

The father appeared, shirtless, flat bat in one arm, rake in the other. He handed the bat to his daughter. They exchanged silent instructions and hugs and kisses on the cheek. The father pushed me out the way. Juna yelled for me to run, again and again. I couldn't. I tried to wiggle my toes—nothing, except tiny needles moving up my legs.

Father and daughter forced the white boys into the parking lot. I watched the standoff continue.

"Go back to your desert!"

"Jobs! Not hummus!"

"I'm a Marine!"

"He's a Marine!"

"You killed his brother!"

"You killed my sister!"

"You stole my father!"

"George Washington!"

"No terror!"

"Freedom isn't free!"

"Al-Qaeda!"

"Bin Laden!"

"Radical Islam!"

"Islam!"

"Freedom!"

"Freedom!"

"Freedom!"

"Freedomfreedomfreedomfreedomfreedom!"

"Never forget!"

"What time is it?"

"Freedom time!"

Juna and her father responded with confused fury. The women and their johns still filled the parking lot in various states of undress. They, like me, didn't know what to do or say. Some of them threw rocks and tried to knock the white boys down. Some turned and went back to bed.

After a few minutes, a woman in a baby-blue negligee yelled about cops coming, and the women and their johns sprinted to their cars carrying clothes and unzipped bags. It was as if someone had announced the approach of a tornado or nuclear bomb, sure to bring absolute destruction. With beautiful accidental coordination, the parking lot emptied. The white boys ran into the darkness as the sirens echoed down the highway.

Cops.

Janice.

I jogged back to our room.

Janice was spread across the bed, drooling in a real and deep sleep. The smell had deepened, grown in intensity and scope.

Through our curtains, I spied Juna and her father standing in the same place, straight up, frozen, except for the occasional angry tremor moving up their spines.

"What are you doing?" Janice asked, with her eyes half open.

"The white boys came," I said.

"I don't know what that means," Janice said.

"The cops are coming," I said.

Janice jolted upright. She ran into the bathroom and slammed the door.

"They're not taking us alive," Janice yelled through a tiny hole above the doorknob.

"They're not here for us," I said.

"How do you know?" Janice yelled.

"The white boys," I said.

"I don't know what that means," Janice said.

"They're here," I said.

Juna and her father waved down the cop car. I recognized the cop from Martin's. She hugged Juna and her father. She shook her head as Juna gesticulated. She patted the father's back when he shrunk into the curb and quivered and sobbed.

I joined Janice in the bathroom. She was huddled behind the toilet, small as I'd ever seen her. I motioned for her to join me in the bathtub. We pulled the curtain.

"Fuck," I said.

"What?" Janice asked.

"Fuck," I said.

"What?" Janice asked.

"Fuck," I said.

"What?" Janice asked.

"We have to get out of here," I said.

"I know," Janice said.

We stayed in the tub for I don't know how long. I waited for a knock at our door. I waited for the end.

At some point, when the sky outside the bathroom's tiny window turned a pleasant shade of fire, I closed my eyes. I squinted and buried my regrets and fears. I didn't want to think about my current situation.

Before I drifted off, I saw a pleasant Saturday morning, mist over a disheveled front lawn. I saw myself taking my coffee to a lawn mower. I heard my children yelling for me to hurry up, they were late for soccer, for ballet, for a playdate with our neighbors. I saw day turn to night. I heard Janice yelling for me to come upstairs, get off the couch, get into bed, love her. And I did. And I drifted off.

Mom stood on a mist puff, looking down at me and the earth, holding a suitcase. Had her lips always puffed like that? And her ears, pointed at the tip and round at the bottom, sticking out like tiny wings—my lips, my ears. All this dust, she said. She turned toward me and her thick eyebrows—my eyebrows—turned into butterflies. This room, she said. This room is a mess, she said.

The mist turned into an old Cadillac. I was in the backseat and Mom had the windows cracked. I noticed the highway: a long stretch of sick wheat and brown corn stalks. In all my dreams about her, there was never smoke. Why was there smoke now? Claude, she said through the rearview mirror, butterflies still there, her face, my face, older now. You're a man, she said. The smoke was coming from an arm-length cigarette. She lit another one. There aren't two ways to get where you're going, she said. You're going, she said, the only place you can.

We pulled into Grandma's living room. Grandma's hair was black and her body was full. She shadowboxed on the couch. She beat the air to pieces. The scene shattered around us. Back on the highway: dark. Mom refused to put her headlights on. Mr. Strongman, she said. I look at you and see a mouse, she said. Mr. Strongman the mouse, she said.

I'm not a mouse, I said.

At least you're not your father, she said.

I'm not a mouse, I said. I'm not my father, I said. I'm not my mother, I said. I'm not a runaway, I said. I hang around. I help.

Our old Cadillac with black leather seats didn't have a roof. There were stars out here, constellations that didn't exist. Michael Jordan was up there playing one-on-one with Michael Jackson for charity. The moon wasn't a basketball. She screamed at me through the rearview mirror; her butterflies turned into hawks, flew away with squealing mice in their talons.

Mom disappeared.

Blink: Sixty-Third Street beach facing Lake Michigan, a party laughing out there on the water, on a sinking barge.

Wake up, Claude. Wake up.

Blink: a raft far from shore.

More constellations underwater: Chester Dexter chasing down a moving train, pumping his legs, gaining speed. Renaissance, the conductor, telling him to jump, catch up—fly, fly. Jonah too, in the darkness, shining, floating, bigger than everyone else, above me, silent, benevolent. Simone, Whitney, Connie, and Kenneth beneath me, stuck in thick weeds, waving up—come on, come on, come down, stay here. In another current, far away, Bubbly and Nugget just wanted to say hello, see how I am doing.

Wake up.

Claude.

Blink: Paul beating a pot and pan together. His opened robe. His lucky Purple Rain boxers.

Wake up. Come on. Claude.

Blink: Janice, hiding in plain sight, behind a skinny tree in an open field.

Claude. Come on. Wake up.

Blink: Grandma wiggling on a crowded dance floor, swinging her hips, smoking a cigar, waving goodbye, kicking her feet above a handsome man's head, cracking up, breaking down.

WAKE UP.

WHEN I OPENED my eyes, Janice had her palm raised in the air, poised to slam downward into my face. She was sitting on the edge of the bathtub wearing fresh clothes and makeup.

"What are you doing?" I asked

"Wake the fuck up," Janice said.

"I'm up," I said.

"Let's go," Janice said. "It stinks in here. Let's go for a walk."

"What time is it?" I asked.

"Morning," Janice said. "Early. A new day. Let's seize it."

"We can't do anything reckless," I said.

"You can use my toothbrush," Janice said. "Your breath stinks."

"That cop," I said. "Those white boys. We should leave this place."

"Just for a morning," Janice said, "I want to forget about doom."

I agreed and got ready. Janice took some bills out of the duffel bag and tossed it back in the closet.

"Are you bringing your phone?" I asked.

"I turned it off," Janice said. "Broke it in half and smashed it to bits with a Bible."

Outside, on this new day, we found Juna and her father standing in the parking lot, crying together. The white boys had come back at some point, after the cops went away. There was a pile of sand at their feet, about two feet high. At the mound's summit, a small banner was planted with the words *Sandniggers Go Home* scribbled on it in red marker.

"Why?" Juna asked.

"Why?" her father asked.

And, it seemed, they would've kept asking for eternity, if Janice hadn't interrupted.

"Someone should kill those fuckers," Janice said.

"They're idiots," Juna said, regaining herself. "They will get themselves killed."

"The cops don't know what to do," the father said.

"They're coming back," Juna said.

She looked at Janice and me with understanding and pity. She knew about us; she knew there was something she didn't know about us. I wondered what possibilities were running through her head. I wondered how wrong she was.

"They're coming back, now," she repeated.

Janice and I took our cue, headed away from downtown, toward the outskirts.

Fringes

//////////////////////////

WHEN I BROKE down the white boys to Janice, as we headed onto a wooded trail, she stopped and told me to wait a minute.

"That type of thing still happens?" Janice asked.

"I saw it," I said.

"Why aren't those people in jail?" Janice asked.

"I don't know," I said.

Of course, I knew. I understood the difference between how society treats misbehaving white teenagers and misbehaving black teenagers. Those parties on frat row: broken windows, puke and human shit on the sidewalk, broken bottles, loud bad music and cheap cigarette smoke polluting the night air, those cops showing up and offering warning—just turn it down, bring it inside; those black kids arrested for smoking weed in a parking lot. Those cashiers in the campus grocery store looking at me walking down the candy aisle; those white students pocketing beer cans without hesitation. I could've told Janice why those people weren't in jail and would never see jail. I could've told her all the bad things about Chicago are present around the world in varied degrees, racist cops in South Shore are a lot like racist cops in Missouri, white boys are the same everywhere, racist social structures loom like malevolent skyscrapers. I thought about Janice's gun. I thought I could use it on the white boys without hesitation. I would've told her if she didn't already know.

"Can you imagine?" Janice asked.

"I know," I said.

"If they tried that shit back home?" Janice asked.

"I know," I said.

The trail was slim and named after a colonel I didn't know. Fallen leaves crunched and squished as we walked. I jumped whenever a squirrel surfaced with a nut. Janice jumped when a dead snake greeted us at a bend. I screamed.

"Why do people like this?" Janice asked.

"Walking around?" I asked.

"Walking around in this." Janice pointed down the leaf-strewn path protected by shedding trees. Green, orange, red, and brown blended into a pleasant sight, I guess, for most people.

"The fresh air," I reasoned. "I understand the fresh air. Nothing else makes sense."

"Just look at that." Janice pointed at a bird, dead, on its back, with flies circling around its tiny talons.

I looked away.

"Everything is dead," I said.

"That," Janice continued. "That is going to kill us all."

We continued on in sustained panic and unease. We collected ourselves on a bench overlooking a dried-up river.

WE FOUND RUNNING water, up the trail, bubbling out of a hole and sliding down a tiny hill. We stared at the hole, waited for it to tell us something about gravity and falling and miracles and freedom.

"Let's get out of here," Janice said to me, while keeping her eyes on the bubbling hole.

"Yes," I said. "Please."

The trail brought us back to the start.

"Where should we go?" Janice asked.

"The moon," I said.

"That doesn't help," Janice said. "Your jokes aren't funny."

"We can't go back to the motel," I said. "The cops might still be there."

On the curb of an unknown road, we looked in every direction for an exit. Between a set of thin clouds, I caught pieces of the moon. Up there, I thought. Why not, I thought.

WE FOUND A neglected dog park after walking for an hour. Flaking piles of dog shit hid under fallen leaves. A mangled squirrel was decomposing at the edge of a small pond. Janice saw the water from outside the fence.

Like tumbleweeds, balls of fur floated across dying grass. We were alone and, for the moment, hidden. We sat at a picnic table, underneath an old tree stripped of leaves and bark, gathered our thoughts.

"When I was little," I said, "all my friends disappeared. They all went away."

"Me too," Janice said.

"And then you," I said. "And you found me down here."

"I hate it down here," Janice said.

"I thought you'd run away from me," I said.

"Why would you think that?" Janice asked.

"Everybody does," I said.

"Don't act depressed," Janice said. "It's not a good look for you. Are you going to cry? Don't cry. Don't make everything worse."

I stopped myself from crying.

"Before you came down here, I don't know what I would've done. I missed you."

Something troubled the tiny pond's surface. We missed the action, just saw ripples expand and crash into the shore.

"I missed you too," Janice said. "I'm sorry about all this."

"What were you thinking?" I asked.

Janice slid closer to me. I put my head on her shoulder, my hand on her knee; I exhaled into her neck. She curled her arm around my head, cradled my head in her bicep; if she wanted to, she could've snapped my neck. I was at her whim.

"Where should we go?" Janice asked.

"Remember?" I asked. "When we used to have these conversations? About running away?"

"This is for real," Janice said.

"I know," I said. "I'm happy."

"What about Florida?" Janice asked.

"What about India?" I asked.

"How would we get there?" Janice asked.

"I'm just thinking out loud," I said.

"This is serious," Janice said.

A large white dog shot into sight, sprang into the water. In happy delirium, it paddled in a circle and snapped its large teeth at the turbulent wake. A short white-haired woman with a messy ponytail strolled to the shore, applauded her dog's excitement. She didn't notice us until we stood up.

"Where's your dog?" She yelled at us, even though a whisper would've sufficed. She tensed her shoulders, looked uncomfortable.

"We lost our dog in a tornado!" Janice yelled back.

"Oh, no!" the woman yelled. She shook her head and ponytail.

"He was a beautiful baby!" Janice yelled.

"God bless you!" the woman yelled. She went back to applauding—her dog had found the rotting squirrel, ripped it like a sock.

Janice and I made our way to the exit, careful to avoid shit and other lifeless flotsam.

Grandma called me. We were at a gas station. Janice was trying to use the bathroom without buying anything.

"Speakerphone," Grandma said. "Paul's here."

"What's up?"

"You tell me what's up," Grandma said. "What the hell did you do?"

"What type of shit tsunami have you conjured?" Paul asked.

"What are you talking about?" I asked.

"Baby," Grandma said, "they came here."

"To our house," Paul said. "They came to our house."

"They had guns," Grandma said.

"They stole our fancy plates," Paul said.

"They wanted Janice," Grandma said.

"They told us about a wedding," Paul said.

"They told us their friends were arrested," Grandma said.

"You ruined their good time," Paul said.

"Someone tipped them off," Grandma said.

"Some got away," Paul said.

"They know it was Janice," Grandma said.

"They put a gun in your grandmother's face," Paul said.

"They punched Paul in the stomach," Grandma said.

"They tied us up with old towels," Paul said.

"We just got free," Grandma said.

"Is she with you?" Paul asked.

"What kind of nonsense are you two peddling?" Grandma asked.

"She's in the bathroom," I said.

"Baby," Grandma said, "they're coming for you. They know where you are."

"They're riding chariots of death," Paul said.

"What were you *thinking*?" Grandma asked.

Both of them were out of breath. As they collected themselves, I closed my eyes and considered walking in front of an 18-wheeler headed toward the highway at high speed.

"Are you there?" Paul asked.

"Yes," I said, and stepped back from the street.

"Are you afraid?" Grandma asked.

"Yes," I said.

"You can't come here," Grandma said.

"You got to go somewhere better," Paul said.

"They're coming for you," Grandma said.

"And they're going to find you," Paul said.

"Are you there?" Grandma asked.

"I think so," I said.

"We love you," Paul said.

"You fools," Grandma said. "We love you."

I wanted to ask if I would see them again, somewhere, anywhere. I wanted to say thank you and I love you and I hope you forgive me. The right thing to say spun at an unreachable distance, just over there, behind my eyes, over my head. They knew me. They loved me. They wanted me to survive. They would find me wherever I was. I pictured them both hunched over the phone, bruised, shaken, standing firm, South Shore buzzing outside their windows, a bus heading downtown, a bus heading further south; I pictured Chicago and all its divisions revealed, at once, in a complicated ballet.

"I love you too," I said.

"You better," Paul said.

"How much time do we have?" I asked.

"They're coming," Grandma said. "They could be close."

"I'll talk to you soon," I said.

"Don't you get it?" Paul asked. "You don't think I sit up late at night? Don't I sound tired? Don't I sound busted up? If I knew how to raise you better—don't you think I would've tried? I look back at my life and think it's okay. I'm alive, still. I'm not dead yet. My only regret is what I showed you, the example I set. You deserved better. Don't you know that? Don't you understand?"

"Baby," Grandma said, "don't get yourself killed."

We fumbled through more declarations of love. They didn't cry, so I didn't cry.

Janice found me on the curb.

"Somehow," Janice said, "someone pissed on the doorknob and sink and paper towels and trash can."

She took a closer look at me, pulled me up.

"What's wrong?" she asked. "Wait. What's wrong?"

WE HID BEHIND some trees and a bus stop. I called information and asked for Loka House. The man laughed when I told him it was an emergency.

"I always move fast," the man said.

Janice memorized the number when I repeated it. She closed her eyes and moved her lips fast, not wanting a digit to slip away.

"Juna?" I asked when Juna picked up.

"Who is this?" Juna asked.

"Are the cops still there?" I asked.

"You better hurry," Juna said. "They're coming back tonight."

WE HURRIED AND tried to figure out our future.

"We'll take the bus," I said. "Out west."

"We'll take a bus to a plane," Janice said.

"Then a plane to a boat," I said.

"Europe," Janice said.

"Africa," I said.

"South America," Janice said. "Peru. Argentina. Uruguay."

"India," I said. "Mumbai."

We went on like that: naming places between our heavy breaths, making sharp turns, hurdling fire hydrants, squeezing through confused people, worried people, people unsure what to make of a young black couple running, smiling, naming destinations. Maybe they were happy for us; happy we were leaving. Or, maybe, they wanted to join us, chase our dream. What is certain is that anyone watching Janice and me bounding like that—weightless—would never guess what we were running from.

Juna waved us down in the parking lot. We didn't break speed, just ran into the main office.

"Hurry," Juna said. "Hurryhurryhurryhurry."

She opened the door to the backroom, ushered us in, locked the locks, and turned on the lights.

I was expecting a storage room in shambles, a dark place. Instead, my feet rested on lush carpet. The room was small, yes. Still, the walls were a gentle cream. There was a small bed with folded sheets and fluffed pillows on one side of the wall. The opposite side was filled with small and medium TV screens. The small screens, like cracker boxes, transmitted scenes from the parking lot, from ten different angles—nothing, at the moment. The medium screens, two of them, both cracked, displayed cricket matches I didn't understand. On the back wall, another door, this one made of metal and locked with thick metal beams.

"Tell me," Juna said. "Did you kill anyone?"

"No," I said.

"You are not on the run for murder?" Juna asked.

"No," I said.

Juna seemed to relax. She wanted to test her own limits for compassion. Would she, I wondered, hold us captive until the cops came if we had committed murder?

"Okay," Juna said. "Father is getting your stuff from your room."

"Who are you to touch our stuff?" Janice asked.

"What is going on?" I asked.

"They came," Juna said.

"Who?" Janice asked.

"No," I said.

"Men with guns," Juna said. "Two men with two guns."

Janice and I sat on the carpet. Juna took the bed. On the screens, nothing continued to happen.

"I thought we had more time," I said.

"I'm sorry," Janice said. "I'm sorry I got us all killed."

"They had a beautiful picture of you," Juna said to Janice.

"What did you tell them?" Janice asked.

"I didn't tell them anything," Juna said. "My father thought they were your friends."

"Friends with guns!" Janice screamed.

Juna looked prepared to make a passionate defense of her father's judgment. She clutched her jaw in familial devotion.

Then we heard the locks unlocking, grunting on the other side. We all climbed into the bed.

The father burst in and tossed the bag at us.

He locked the locks and slid to the carpet. Sweat flowed down his wrinkles into his shirt.

Waiting

THE BEST THING—THE only thing—to do was wait until nightfall. Then, we figured, Juna could drop us at the bus station. Nightfall was six hours away. Janice sat on the duffel bag. I was at her feet, prone, trying to sleep. Juna and her father cheered in whispers at the cracked screens.

"I don't get it," Janice said. "Is it like baseball?"

"Yeah," Juna said, without looking back. "Sort of."

"If I explained," the father said, "you wouldn't understand."

"I didn't ask you," Janice said to the father's head. In misplaced anger, Janice kicked my ribs.

Time passed in strange bursts.

Hour One

"So, are you two a couple?"

"Not really."

"It's hard to explain."

"You seem in love."

"A lot has happened to us."

"And this is only the beginning."

Hour Two

Janice slid off the duffel bag, tried to sleep next to me. She fitted her body into mine. Then we got too hot, started sweating. I rolled over; she rolled over, put her arm around my waist. Then we got hotter, sweated more. We both rolled onto our backs. I put my sweating right hand into her sweating left hand. Then we got hotter, inched our bodies apart, kept our sweating hands interlocked, stayed like that until I felt a powerful urge to cry. I took my hand from Janice's, rubbed my eyes, rolled on my side, showed her my back. She rolled over too, put an arm around my waist, held me tight. Then we got hotter and stayed like that.

Hour Two and a Quarter

Nothing on the small screens.

Hour Three

"The bus will take you to Kansas City. Where will you go from there?"

"We could stay in Kansas City?"

"No one stays in Kansas City."

"We could keep going west?"

"Am I crazy?"

"For not liking Kansas City?"

"No. For leaving this behind."

"Leaving what behind?"

"The newspaper. My work. School. A planned-out future."

"We'll have each other," Janice said. "We'll plan a future."

"I could write a story about this."

"I need you."

"I need you too."

"After Kansas City, we'll keep going."

"Keep going where?"

"Anywhere."

"Anywhere isn't a place."

"Everywhere."

"Janice . . ."

"Claude . . ."

Hour Four

Simone called. I didn't answer.

Hour Four and Three Minutes

Whitney called. I didn't answer.

Hour Four and Twenty Minutes

Connie Stove called and left a voice mail. I listened while trying to balance a plastic cup on my chin. Janice slept with her head in my lap. The father slept with his feet in Juna's lap. Juna slept with her head against a screen.

"You don't pick up now," Connie Stove's voice began, "you must have your reasons. You might feel slighted, used and abused. You might feel slighted because you are an individual and we're treating you like a token, our token black person, our urban voice and mind. You might feel anger now and I understand your anger. I have felt your anger. I too was a token, am a token.

"You'll pretend it's okay. You'll hope it's okay. They'll give you an office. They'll give you a parking spot. They'll call you esteemed. They'll let you come to lunch when the donors are in town. They'll ask you to speak at Commencement, Diversity Day, Family Weekend, Homecoming. They'll ask you to help write a commercial for the university and you'll do it. You'll do all of it. You'll do all of it and smile and the smile will mean nothing.

"You'll look back at those years and you'll call them golden. Those years spent running up stairs, down hallways, between desks. Those years spent listening to your instincts. Your instincts did you well; they served you. You could walk into a maze and find your way out, eyes closed, just using your gut. You traced that feeling in your gut, once, high on mushrooms in Idaho with Kissinger and Rumsfeld. You traced that feeling in your gut to your soul. You'll look back at the night outside Boise, near the waterfalls, under big sky. You'll look back at those years and you'll call them wasted. All that. For what?"

Hour Five

"So, there's the bowler. And there's two batters."

"The bowler is like a pitcher?"

"Yes. Except a bowler can only throw six pitches at a time."

"That's stupid."

"It's called an over."

"And that's a home run?"

"We call them sixes."

"Why?"

"It's worth six points. And that's a four."

"Why?"

"It's worth four points."

"Why?"

"Because it hit the boundary."

"I don't understand."

"Me neither."

"Wait, wait, wait, wait—what's that?"

"Another six."

"No, no, no, no—on the other screen. LOOK!"

There was movement on all the small screens. Black cars, large and imposing, converged on the parking lot. In seconds, the lot was filled, each spot taken. Then, like a movie, we watched as the doors opened and men stepped out, one by one, two by two. They carried blunt instruments and firepower.

In the following seconds, the four of us tried to react to what was unfolding. We each stopped at a gasp and moan.

Finally, Janice forced something through her fear, which, if it was like my fear, was enough to make you pray for quick death.

"Of course," Janice said. "It's a fucking ghost."

Janice pointed at one of the screens, held her shaking finger inches away from the only person not carrying a weapon.

"No," I said.

"Yes," Janice said.

"It can't be," I said.

"It is," Janice said. "I would never forget."

That person walking on the screen. That person jumping onto the hood of an especially tall truck. That person shouting words we couldn't hear; threats, I think. That person wasn't a ghost. That person was death.

"Big Columbus," I said.

"Big Columbus," Janice said.

"What's a Big Columbus?" the father asked.

Nightfall

////////////////////////////////

IN OUR IMMEDIATE and total panic, Janice and I paced around the room and prayed for guidance. After some brief negotiation, we decided to call the cops and tell them everything.

"Yes," I said. "They are here now and they are going to kill us."

We had reached the point of drowning. The shit was at our necks and rising with unpredictable speed.

"You didn't tell us it was an army," Janice said to Juna, shaking.

"It wasn't," Juna said. "It was only two guys. Look. What are they doing? Look!"

From the screens, we watched as the Redbelters moved with regimented precision, split into groups, busted into motel rooms, looking for us.

"The cops are coming," Juna said. "The cops are coming."

"What a way to go," the father said.

Big Columbus, from his perch, orchestrated the raid. He got a signal from a henchman, a nod signaling we weren't anywhere to be found, I think. Big Columbus moved toward the main office. He moved toward us, his pack close behind.

"They don't know we're in here," Juna said.

The father took his shirt off.

"What are you doing?" Juna asked.

"If I'm going down," the father said, as he pulled a cricket bat from underneath the bed, "I'm going down swinging."

And the world slowed down. I watched Big Columbus and his men on a screen walk into the main office. All that kept us from them was a door and locks. When death is certain, your life doesn't replay in any organized fashion—a smooth film doesn't run in your mind. In that moment, I didn't see Mom and Dad fighting in Lake Michigan. I didn't see myself crying when they left. I didn't see Grandma holding me, crying too, in her quiet and imperceptible way. I didn't see Paul standing in his bathrobe in the kitchen with a goblet of wine and pan of burned bacon. I didn't see Jonah, Bubbly, Nugget, Chester Dexter, or Renaissance. I didn't see any minor characters walk onstage and demand appreciation. I didn't see the riot. I didn't see my neighborhood burning, with Big Columbus rubbing ashes between his palms.

I did see myself above Lake Michigan, flying, smiling into the gray and green shore. I was high above and removed from earthbound horrors. That's what I felt; that's what I saw: Chicago and South Shore far away, out of reach. And Janice was next to me, flying and happy and holding my hand as menacing clouds flew in our direction.

Back on earth, Janice wrapped her arms around my waist, kept me grounded. And I wrapped my arms around her.

Big Columbus banged on the door.

"We have come for our revenge," Big Columbus said. "We have come for justice. And we will take it."

The father stood close to the door, shirtless and armed and unmoved. He gave us a look like he was ready to meet the horde head on.

In Juna, I saw Grandma, as the riot bore down on our house, ready to maim. I saw fire blossoming from her hair. Her unflappable body produced a golden silhouette.

Cops. Lots of cops. Lines of cops pulling into the parking lot.

THERE IS SOME debate between us regarding what Big Columbus said before charging his men into the horrific, medieval melee.

Juna heard, "Let's fucking do this."

The father heard, "Now is our time."

Janice heard, "This time we conquer."

I'm not sure what I heard. My ears were too filled with blood. There was this pounding behind my ears that took days to disappear.

Either way, Big Columbus and his Redbelters left us alone and met the cops. We watched it unfold, for a few minutes, in our backroom, on small screens, with cricket playing on bigger screens. It's impossible to know who fired the first shot, who threw the first blunt instrument at the enemy. I had seen it all before, and I still didn't know what to make of the violence, the hate, the dropping bodies, and the screams. It was instant warfare. In a parking lot. In a small Missouri town.

"Not again," Janice. "Not again, not again, not again."

I pulled her face into mine. Our eyelashes touched. She was so close I couldn't see her.

"It's not the same," I said. "It's not the same."

"Now," Juna said.

I kept hold of Janice and grabbed the duffel bag; Juna grabbed her father.

The gun. I could have taken Janice's gun. I could have faced Big Columbus. I could have faced them down and pulled the trigger. I could have died for all of Big Columbus's victims.

Janice gripped my hand.

I made a choice.

We escaped into chaos, out the back door, into Juna's car, out into a new world.

We drove past the brutal conflict, heard screams and more sirens and more screams. Confederate flags appeared up the street.

"You're kidding me," Juna said.

The white boys paused their pickup trucks at a stop sign, idled, and didn't move. Juna pulled up next to them, rolled down her window. Behind us, in front of them—guns popping. All around, the sirens closed in on the white boys.

We left them as we found them: scared shitless.

From the highway, we saw billowing smoke filled with blood and sparks.

Sunrise

////////////////////////

WE RODE UNTIL we needed gas. Then, we rode some more. Kansas passed our window; Colorado took us into clouds and snow. Somewhere in Utah, between Mormon hideouts, I asked Juna to pull over so I could vomit the adrenaline out. The father spoke of his life's work, ruined, states behind us. He spoke of respect and decency. Juna told him to turn up the radio—they were talking about Big Columbus. Everywhere, they were talking about Big Columbus and his Redbelters and Loka House. A commentator compared Loka House to South Shore and the Redbelters to Al-Qaeda. This time, the authorities said, Big Columbus was done, shot in a motel parking lot. His Redbelters were done. Civilization could sleep easier, they said.

Watching the mountains dip outside my window like animate massive portraits, I thought about what Big Columbus wanted. He wanted a place for his people. He wanted his life to make sense. I understood that.

The radio mentioned four missing people, presumed dead. They didn't say much else. It was all burned down.

Juna rolled down the windows and let Nevada's sunrise spill into the car. We pulled over in the desert. I pulled the gun from the bag. I threw as far as I could, which wasn't far at all.

They agreed to take us to the ocean. After the ocean, who knew?

Where We Belong

///

SOMETIMES, WHEN IT'S morning and we're both tired, I stare across the table and see Janice again in Juna's backseat.

I see her hair rattling in the wind. I feel my hand on her knee, held there for hours and miles.

I see her on the beach, picking up empty shells. I hear her kicking sand. I smell salt on her shoulders.

I turn to her whenever the future frightens me, the present frightens me, the past ambushes my peace, and sleep doesn't come.

When the sun rises and Janice looks right at me, I see them all in her eyes. Grandma and Paul, happy, laughing, waving—safe; everyone in South Shore, safe and happy. They're okay without us. They forgive us for leaving.

We're okay too.

Yes. Right where we belong.

ACKNOWLEDGMENTS

THANK YOU, FAMILY: Mom, Dad, Mike, Nat, Chris, Grandpa, Grandma; Oklahoma cousins, uncle, and aunt; Harlem cousins, uncles, and aunt; Uncle Jim.

Thank you, Chicago family: Jer, Jon, Ted, Cynthia, Nate, Alex, Mike Case, Rich, Tim, Schutz, Ben, Pat, Don, Addie, Ciara, Lexie, Isa, Lex, Laura, Andrew, Julia, Wendy, James, Cleaves, Scoop, Tracy, Jay, Rah, J-Woo, DP.

Thank you, Halie.

Thank you, Theoharides family. Thank you, Costello family. We miss you, Alex.

Thank you, Sojourner.

Thank you, University of Chicago Laboratory Schools folks.

Thank you, University of Missouri folks.

Thank you, School of the Art Institute folks.

Thank you, University of Massachusetts folks.

Thank you, patient teachers: Ruth Golb, Wayne Brasler, Charles Brahnam, Jess Bowers, Mark Booth, Todd Hasak-Lowy,

Janet Desaulniers, Jenny Magnus, James McManus, Sabina Murray, Edie Meidav, Noy Holland, Arthur Flowers.

Thank you, brilliant classmates: Clare O'Connor, Alena Saunders, Ann Ward, Chelsea Hogue, Laura Warman, Brendan Bowles, Jane Dykema, Chris Lott, Zoe Mungin, Liza Birnbaum.

Thank you, Care Center. Thank you, Holyoke.

Thank you, Studio Paris.

Thank you, Disquiet International Literary Program.

Thank you, Algonquin Books.

Thank you, Lisboa.

Thank you, Harlem.

Thank you, Buffalo.

Thank you, South Shore. Love you.

Thank you, Alexa Stark.

Thank you, Kathy Pories.

Thank you, Adam Levin.

Thank you, Jeff Parker. Love you, dog.

Thank you, Dr. Grace Gibson.

Thank you, Caitlin.

Thank you, Hoot. Thank you, Frank.

You all make life worth living. You all brought me here.